THE
COMPLEX
LEADER

Book Three of THE COMPLEX TRILOGY

HEATHER HAYES

First soft back edition December 2018

Published by AH Digital FX Studios, INC 12/12/2018
AH Digital FX Studios, INC
10551 E. Ririe Hwy.
Idaho Falls, ID 83401
www.ahfx.net

ISBN: 978-1-945597-08-4

Library of Congress Control Number: 2018967039

Cover by Adam Hayes
Book Layout & Design by Adam Hayes

Paperback printed in United States of America

For Sarah and Logan
It is a rare gift when family and friends
are one and the same.

Chapter 1

THE ITCHINESS OF MY WIG is going to drive me crazy. I've scratched my head at least 50 times in the last two hours. I resist the urge to scratch again so I don't blow my cover.

A loud, male voice directs my attention to the stage of the Grand Hotel's banquet hall. "And the winner of the Herrington Vote-Off is—Brock Hamble!" My smiling, political brother cordially shakes hands with his opponent, Leonard Bloxhouse, and joins the handsome master of ceremonies at the microphone to wave to the crowd.

I jump out of my seat in the midst of thousands of other

people and shout for joy. Garth is only a second behind me when he gets to his feet and kisses me, bumping his big, fake nose into mine. "This plan is going to work, Elira. I can feel it."

I whisper into his ear, "I think our plan will work too, but I don't want to get cocky. Just because Herrington is voting for Brock doesn't mean all of the cities will."

My father leans over to us. "Winning this Vote-Off brings him up to 60% of the popular vote. Things are looking good for us."

I smile with relief. If my brother, Brock, wins the senate seat, he will propose a change to our archaic law that keeps people with physical flaws locked away in the complex. "How many days are left until the official vote?"

Dad rubs his hands together. "Eight."

Those eight days can't get here soon enough. I turn to my other, less-political brother, Greggory. "When are you going to air the footage at the news station of what's really doing on in the complex?"

"Right after Brock wins it. So probably ten days from now. Hey, here comes Charlie."

A short, stocky man with a big video camera approaches us. "Doctor Hamble, I'm Charlie Jessen from the national news station. You are the father of Brock Hamble, are you not? I'd like to interview you for a piece I'm putting together about Brock for tomorrow's news."

My father smiles as he shifts his feet. "Uh, sure. That's fine."

Charlie nods to my mother's turned back. "We will want to see your lovely wife showing her support too."

Mother turns around and smiles in her bedazzling way. "I would love to tell the world about the best future senator the United Cities has ever seen."

Charlie turns and smiles at Garth and me. "Excellent. Would your guests like to say a few words in favor of Brock Hamble on the news as well?"

Fear surges through my veins. "No! No, thank you," I say at the same time as Garth. "We are late for a meeting with—a sponsor. We'll see you later, Doctor Hamble." I give my father a knowing look as I shake his hand.

"See you later, Josie. Remember that number we talked about." He tries not to look worried about us as he turns to my brother. "Greggory, you should join us on the other side of the camera for once. We want to show the country how excited Brock's family is to see him pulling ahead in the polls." I feel myself twitch.

Greggory shows a new side of himself when he smiles and claps Charlie on the back. "Sure, anything for my old pal, Charlie, here."

Great—this interview will probably take forever, and we just claimed we were leaving. How are we going to get home? It took quite a bit of convincing to get my parents to let me come here tonight. I need to prove to them that I know how to get myself out of uncomfortable situations. Garth intertwines his fingers with mine as we leave the Grand Hotel's banquet hall. We always walk so his normal hand is on the side next to me, so we can do this. His deformed hand is safely hidden in his pocket. He tilts his head toward the hotel desk. There is a telephone sitting on it. I haven't used the telephone very much, but Ernestine made us all memorize my parents' phone number in case we ever need help. I guess this is as much a time for help as any.

Garth points at the telephone. "Your dad did mention a number we talked about."

I scratch my chin nervously. "I'm sure you're right. I hope I can do this."

The lady at the desk smiles at us, completely clueless that she is looking at two wanted persons. "May I help you?"

I smile sweetly at her. "May we use your phone, please?"

"Sure. Just dial nine and then the number."

My finger shakes as I try not to mess up the phone number. The voice on the other end sounds like Ernestine trying to disguise her voice to sound like a man. "Hello? Hamble residence."

"We need a ride back from The Grand Hotel. Are you available?"

"Yep. On my way." I hang the phone up, relieved that our solution will work.

4

I see a woman with spikey blonde hair and a big, round stomach across from me. She is going to have a baby! I've never seen someone this pregnant so close-up before. I feel myself drawn to her. Before Garth can stop me, I touch the woman's protruding stomach. "You have a baby growing inside of you. How wonderful."

The woman pats my arm and smiles at me like I'm the cutest 10-year-old she's ever seen. "Yes. There is a baby growing inside of me. Thanks for noticing." I smile one more time and back away, embarrassed.

Garth walks me away from the crowd of people. "You probably shouldn't have touched her stomach."

I feel silly now for doing it. "Yeah, you're probably right." I turn around and see the woman giving me a weird look as she whispers to her husband. "I hope Ernestine gets here soon. I feel so stupid."

Ernestine definitely doesn't obey the speed limit getting here, but I'm grateful that we don't have to wait outside with these people for long. Dressed like a man with a hat and mustache, she rolls down the window and asks, "Did you two order a ride?"

"Yes, we did. Thank you," I say as we slip inside the black car.

Ernestine doesn't turn around as she drives off. "Well?"

I smile. "He won. That puts him to 60% of the popular vote."

"Perfect. I need to stop by Complex Supplies Row on our way home, if that's all right."

My smile turns into a frown. "Ugh. I hate that place. Why?"

"Maxine said she had to drive the linen truck to the storefront tonight because the complex is so short-handed right now, and she had information she didn't want to say over the phone."

I shrug. "Okay." I am amazed that Maxine is doing so many weird jobs for the complex these days. She used to take care of my age-group of girls only. I wonder what kind of news she can have that she doesn't want to share over the phone.

Garth sees the worry in my eyes. "It'll be okay. Don't be anxious."

My nerves are on edge more than ever since my best friend was captured and taken back to the Complex of Undesirables. "It might be news about Avra in the complex." Garth takes my hand and nods understandingly.

When we pull up to Complex Supplies Row, we don't see a supply truck anywhere. Stores line the street on both sides, filled with goods our friends who are imprisoned in the complex are forced to make with no pay. It's 9:00 at night and all the shopkeepers are turning the signs in their windows from 'Open' to 'Closed.' I try not to sweat as I see the pretty linen shopkeeper stacking pillowcases by color in her window display. One of those might have been made by me on a job research day during my own time in the complex. Or, maybe one of them is the one Bicep sewed before pounding the table and sending his sewing machine crashing to the floor. He'll never know that what he sewed made money for someone else.

Urch. The sound of loud brakes interrupts my thoughts. Maxine looks out of place as she climbs out of the huge, white, covered truck that she has somewhat successfully parked.

We jump out of our car to join her. "Is there anything you don't do at the complex, Maxine?" I ask.

Maxine looks at us curiously for a minute, but then figures out who we are in our disguises. She wipes sweat off her brow with her jumpsuit sleeve and forces a fake smile on her face. "Well, let's just say, I've dropped a few notches on the totem pole since the break-out."

The side door to the linen shop opens and the pretty worker approaches Maxine. We shut our mouths and return to our car until the linens are unloaded and the worker locks her shop. Once the linen worker drives away in her yellow sports car, Maxine approaches our car.

My favorite adult and confidant from the complex avoids eye contact with me when she approaches us. "May I have a private word with you, Ernestine?"

Ernestine nods her head wearily. "Sure. You two—stay out of trouble."

"What do you consider trouble?" Garth asks with a wink.

Ernestine gives him a hard look as she follows Maxine down the street toward the city park.

I don't like that Maxine doesn't want to speak in front of us. "Garth, what if something is wrong with Avra or—Jefrey?"

Garth moves the red curls of my wig back behind my ears as his face tenses. "Jef will get what he deserves, and there's nothing we can do about it."

My boyfriend is still angry that his twin brother turned traitor on us complex escapees and Garth didn't even know it. I tilt my head toward him. "Is that how your parents feel?"

Garth's eyes lower to his hands. "No. My mom is heartbroken. I think my hard-nosed dad is even sad that Jef's back in the complex." I take my boyfriend's hand. It must be hard to lose someone who used to be like his other half. His eyes lift slowly. "They're walking back now. I didn't even get a kiss yet." He plants a wet one on me before Ernestine opens her door.

Ernestine hops into the car and watches Maxine drive away. She doesn't say anything as she turns the engine on. I can't handle the suspense. "What did Maxine say?"

Ernestine pulls onto the road slowly. "I don't know if we should talk about it right now. Let's wait until we're with your parents."

I slap the center console in frustration. "No, Ernestine. What is it?"

"They've been torturing Avra since they took her back, so

three weeks now. She hasn't said anything, but she can't take much more. She's unconscious and—she's dying."

Chapter 2

"DAD, I TOLD YOU WE WEREN'T STRANDED. Ernestine picked us up. I don't care about driving. What I care about is my best friend dying in the complex before we can change the law!" I throw my red, curly wig on the table to prove my point and to let my itchy head breathe.

My father pours himself a tall glass of water and sits down at the other end of the basement table. "Elira, I keep getting the feeling that I need to teach you how to drive. I'm taking you to the desert for driving lessons tomorrow, and that's that."

Garth sits next to him at the table. "May I come too? I really want to drive."

Father shrugs. "Fine. Anyone who wants to learn can come with us."

I stomp my foot in frustration. "Dad, I don't care about driving right now. Avra is dying!" I feel my eyes swell with tears.

My dad stands up and walks around the table to hug me. I wrap my arms around him and let the tears fall. I knew the complex would kill Avra. That's why I got her out of there in the first place. "What are we going to do, Dad? Changing the law will take months, maybe years." I wipe my eyes with my hand before my flesh-colored makeup can stain his shirt.

Father walks back around the table and takes a big drink of water. "I've been thinking about this very thing since they took her back. I have a plan."

"You do?" I smile for the first time since Ernestine got back in the car tonight.

"Yes, but it would mean letting a friend of mine in on our secrets. I've been trying to decide if he would turn you in or not, and—I don't think he would."

My anxious eyes search my dad's face. "Who is he?"

"His name is Henry Ricks. He works for both complexes as—a gravedigger."

I nod my head in acknowledgement. "You've mentioned him before."

Rocky joins us at the table. "What do you mean by both complexes, Doctor Hamble?"

"He buries the dead from both the Herrington Complex of Undesirables and the Herrington Complex for the Elderly. Every major city in the country has two complexes. One for the elderly and one for the deformed and unsightly."

Rocky turns his head so he can hear better with his good ear. "Why would someone who works for the complex want to help us?"

Mother sits across the table from father to join the conversation. Father smiles at her, then turns to Rocky. "Henry's kind of like Maxine. He thinks the system is unfair and wrong. It pays better than his last job, so he sticks it out, but it makes him sick to bury a kid every other day."

I'm confused about how a gravedigger could be helpful. "So, what can he do for Avra? He won't see her till she's—dead."

Father scratches his head. "I will need Maxine to help us too. I have—acquired a substance that when taken orally will render a person unconscious, it slows all bodily function down to the point of making a person appear dead."

Scott stands up from off the couch and starts pacing the great room. "I don't like the sound of that." He stops pacing after a couple of rounds and asks, "What is it called? Is it safe?"

Father smiles weakly. "It's an illegal, foreign drug called sheol. It is not 100% safe—but 90% of people who take it appear dead for two hours and then slowly regain body function for the next eight hours. Ten hours later, the person should be back to normal."

I am shocked that my father has an illegal drug in his possession. "Where did you get it?"

"I—I'm not proud of this, and I don't recommend any of you do it, but it was the only way I could think to get Avra out of the complex. I—I had Greggory buy it from a drug dealer for me."

My mother pushes herself back from the table. "You had Greggory buy something from a drug dealer?"

"Calm down, Florence. He isn't as innocent as you'd like to think. He hangs out with the party crowd at the university, and he wants to save Avra too." The look on Scott's face is hard to read.

I am still worried about how bad of shape Avra is in. "So, what if the person is already deathly ill when they take this—substance?"

Father sighs. "Those kinds of people are usually the ones who make up the 10% who don't make it."

Scott starts pacing again, this time faster. "It might kill her."

I can see where my dad is heading with this. I jump out of my seat and take Scott's hand to stop his pacing. "Scott, she is dying right now anyway. I think we should at least try to save her."

Garth sees a flaw in the plan. "Maxine doesn't work with the teenage girls anymore, or the troubled kids in private rooms. How will she slip it to her?"

Dad scratches his head. "That's the tricky part of this whole thing. If she can find a way to slip her four drops on Friday around noon, I will be in the complex doing a training for the complex doctors on heart health. I will insist on seeing every patient with heart defects. When they take me to Avra, I will declare her dead and personally assist in putting her in a body bag. I'll help hand her over to Henry, who will then switch that body bag for a body bag filled with rocks and bury that instead."

Why hasn't he marched into the complex sooner? "I didn't know that they let you go inside the complex, Dad."

My father folds his arms across his chest. "You have to be invited, and this is only my second invitation. It's now or never."

We all sit there and think about the implications of the plan before speaking. My mother speaks up first. "Is Henry poor enough to be tempted by a bounty?"

Father scratches his chin. "Well, he isn't wealthy by any means, but he has an adult-onset heart murmur himself. I've been kind enough to keep his secret, and I believe he will be kind enough to keep mine."

Garth scrunches his eyebrows together and asks, "What would happen to Henry if people knew he had a heart murmur?"

Father tilts his head from side to side. "Hopefully nothing. Adult bodies break down as they age, but some employers don't employ people with obvious health problems. They think it reflects bad taste on the company's part."

"Oh."

Mother looks at her watch and purses her lips. "The timing will be tricky. If Maxine gives it to her at noon, you better see her before two."

"I'll be in the complex from 8:00 until 3:00. I'll present my material quickly in the morning, getting done at 10:00, and then see patients until 3:00. There are about 200 heart patients in the complex."

I shake my head in amazement. "Two hundred patients! You'll never get to her in time."

Father reaches a hand out to me in explanation. "Since I'm presenting on heart murmurs, my goal is to identify all the patients who should be on the new heart murmur medicine that just came out. I'll have them send all heart patients to the doctors' office starting with the youngest dorms and ending with the oldest workers in a steady lineup. I only need five minutes per patient to establish if they have a murmur or not. I have a lot of pull in the medical community, so I think the complex doctors will obey my wishes. I promise I'll find a way to see Avra between noon and two."

My mother looks at her watch again. "I will call Maxine and have her meet me at my salon tomorrow to pick up the bottle of sheol. She'll have to do some quick thinking to be where we need her to be on Friday." Mother looks at the ceiling as she thinks. She suddenly snaps her fingers. "She told me she has a little troublemaker in the five-year-old group. Maybe she can bring her to solitary on Friday for bad behavior and offer to help with Avra while she's there."

My heart leaps in my chest. Thank goodness my mother is so smart. "That sounds pretty reasonable, Mom. I know Maxine would do anything to help Avra."

Mom squeezes my hand. "We all would, Elira. Ross, you need to win Henry over by Wednesday so he can arrange to be on duty Friday from noon until two."

Father nods. "I know his shifts are usually 8:00-5:00, because I've stayed late in the office to accommodate his work schedule every time he comes in. So it should work if he's on duty Friday."

Mother's face is serious. "If he seems hesitant, offer him a reward. Avra is worth it."

Father nods his head in agreement. "Henry has been feeding me information about the complex ever since he got the job there. I know he hates what they do, but if a bribe is necessary, I'll do it."

I'm feeling a crunch on time. "Today is Monday; you're taking me driving tomorrow. When will you talk to him, Dad?"

"I will stop by his house after driving lessons tomorrow. He found himself in a predicament without his heart medication a few months ago. He called me, and I brought him some, so I know where he lives. It's one street away from Avra's parents."

I know that the houses in that area belong to people living on the poor side of life. I hope we can trust this guy. A nervous sigh escapes my lips. "It's not a perfect plan, but it's the only plan we've got. I just hope she can hang on until Friday."

Chapter 3

MOTHER TAKES A WET BREAKFAST PLATE from me. "Elira, remember the man who interviewed us at the Vote-Off last night?" she asks.

"Yes," I say as I feel around in the soapy dish water for another plate.

"He introduced us to Brock's Herrington campaign manager, Douglas Shriner. He'll be on the news with us tonight."

I keep washing the breakfast dishes as Mother dries them. "Okay."

"We had a nice chat with Mr. Shriner after our interviews.

He was wondering if we had any family members who could volunteer handing out 'Vote for Hamble' buttons and flyers on Wednesday at the city fair."

"That's tomorrow." I hand my mom a dripping bowl. "You, Dad, and Greggory could."

"Yes—but I had a crazy thought come to me while we were talking to him. I told him that our niece, Edith, would be in town that day and that she might be willing to help. You did so well at the Vote-Off, and I kind of want you to get used to interacting with strangers. What do you think?"

I snicker. "There would be so many people there, surely someone would recognize me."

Mother's eyes become serious. "That's the funny thing about crowds and menial jobs. An individual person can become invisible in that environment."

That is an interesting thought. Sometimes all I want is to be seen and acknowledged; other times, all I want is to be invisible. "Invisible, huh? Do you want me to try it?"

"Yes. You really don't look like that picture they keep putting on the news in your disguises. I think you would learn a lot, without standing out, with so many people and so many booths in one place."

I think of all the sights and sounds that being outside brings to my attention. I realize that I want to be a part of it. "All right. I'll do it. Can Garth come too?"

Mother's eyes narrow. "Isn't he supposed to go to his parents' house for his little brother's birthday tomorrow?"

My shoulders droop. "Oh, yeah. Never mind, I don't want to be alone there, Mom."

Mother nudges me with her shoulder. "Greggory, your dad, and I will all be there with you. Don't be afraid."

I open the drain in the sink and watch the soapy water disappear. "Okay. I do want to get a feel for how many people are really voting for Brock."

Mother claps her hands with excitement. "Perfect, it's all settled then. You, Garth, and Rocky should eat your lunch and get ready for driving lessons in the desert."

"Isn't Scott coming with us?" I worry about him. Losing Avra has made him depressed.

"No. He is going to visit his parents today. He hasn't been back since Avra was taken. Ernestine says the officer surveillance has gone down quite a bit the last couple of days. It's time."

I squeeze the key in my pocket. "It probably is time, but he's going to miss out."

"ELIRA, WATCH OUT FOR THE CACTUS!" my dad yells.

"Ahh!" Too late. I hope my beautiful purple car isn't

scratched up too much on the right side. It's hard to tell how close is too close to certain things on my dad's homemade road consisting of cacti, orange cones, and cardboard box signs.

"She's a woman; give her a break."

I flip around in the driver's seat, nicking the side of an orange cone with my tire in the process. "What's that supposed to mean, Rocky?"

Rocky's eyes open wide as he points ahead to a cardboard box that I bump as well. "Have you seen my mom drive?"

I turn around to face the windshield. "That doesn't mean all women drive like her."

"You're right," Rocky says, and then mutters under his breath, "But you do."

"I heard that."

My dad mops his brow with a handkerchief. "Good job, Elira. It's Garth's turn now. Pull over to the side of the silo and switch spots."

Garth is positively giddy as he jumps out of the back seat. He kisses me on the cheek as he trades me spots. I try not to be jealous as he maneuvers the fake road without running over a cone or sideswiping a cactus.

Rocky leans over and smirks at me. I turn away from him. "Don't say a word, Rocky Moore."

"I wouldn't dream of it."

Rocky gets the last turn. He only hits one cone when he tries to parallel park. His smug look drives me crazy as we stop to have the snacks Freda packed for us. The side of my car creates almost enough shade for the four folding chairs my dad pulls out of the trunk for us.

Father lets out a contented sigh as he pops open a cold soda. "I want each of you to drive the course again when you're done eating. I think we should do this at least once, maybe twice a week until you're ready to drive on your own."

"When will we get to drive on a real road?" Garth asks between bites of chocolate chip cookie.

"You would probably be ready next time we do this, but..." Dad looks sideways at me. "We'll probably stick to the desert for a couple more lessons."

I feel so small as I munch on a celery stick. I am holding these guys back. I used to feel like I was a leader for my friends. The more time goes on, the more I realize that they don't need me. In fact, at times like this, they would probably be better off without me. I bite down on my celery stick again and gag at the grittiness that fills me mouth. I look down at it to see that Rocky has filled my celery with a handful of sand. My face contorts with rage.

Rocky's eyes fill with apprehension. "Ha, ha! It was just a joke, Elira. Your eyes looked like you were off to another planet."

Throwing my celery to the side, I scoop a handful of sand off the ground and jump out of my seat. Rocky takes off running. Luckily my toes have healed since our breakout from the complex, and my adrenaline makes me just a tad faster than Rocky. I tackle him from behind and feed him a mouthful of sand.

"Ugh. Get off me! I won't do it again," Rocky's dark, sandy mouth shrieks.

"You better not," I say as I climb off Rocky's chest.

Garth rushes over and helps dust me off. "You should tackle me next time," Garth whispers in my ear as he dusts off my elbows. I blush as we walk back to my dad.

"With that much determination, you'll be driving like a pro in no time, Elira." My dad is smiling at me, but I see him wipe his brow one last time as we climb back into the car.

After another slightly less eventful round of driving, my dad takes the driver's seat and drives us back to the main road. A rusty, red pick-up truck pulls in right as we're pulling out. A wrinkly old cowboy rolls down his window. "What are you doing here, Dr. Hamble?"

"You said I could teach the troubled youth I volunteer with how to drive out here, remember?"

"Oh, yeah. That's right. If I had a dollar for every charitable thing you've ever done, I'd be a rich man."

"I don't know about that. You're the one letting me use your property. It takes a giving man to do that."

"Well, just keep that in mind when I want you to keep being my doctor once they stick me in The Complex for the Elderly."

"I will. I'll take care of you just like you're taking care of me. Have a good day, Elmer."

"You too, Doc."

I turn around to watch Elmer drive off in the opposite direction. "When is Elmer turning 80?"

"Next year."

"He seems spry enough to take care of himself."

"He is, but once he's 80, he has to obey the law and go to the Complex for the Elderly."

"Do you have to have an invitation to go into the Complex for the Elderly?"

"Not exactly. Doctors are allowed to visit their patients the first Monday of every month, but no one else is able to visit there."

That doesn't seem like enough care for someone with lots of health problems. Some of the girls with red buttons in the complex come to mind. "What if they need their doctors more than that?"

"Then they have to see the complex doctors, and they don't have as much patience as I do."

"Do they have a death doctor?"

"Yes."

I turn around in my seat with a huff. "Hmm. Once Brock is a senator he may want to change that part of the law too."

Chapter 4

"CHECKMATE!" I scream as I knock Rocky's king over. "Take that."

Rocky slaps the sofa in frustration. "I want a rematch. You just got lucky."

"No, I didn't. You just think girls are worse than guys at everything."

Rocky scoffs, "No, I don't."

"Prove it. What am I better at than you?" It takes skill to fish for a compliment while trying to prove a point.

Rocky pauses for a moment as I glare at him. "You got us

out of the complex. I didn't know how to do that. I pay respect where respect is due."

"That's right." I look around the room and see Scott laying his head on the computer desk. "Scott, do you want to play chess? Rocky needs an opponent."

Scott sits up straight and rubs his eyes. "Sure. Why not?"

Rocky shakes his head at me as I smile and walk away. I know I can't beat him twice in a row. He's looking for revenge now. I wander over to the table where Ernestine and Garth are talking quietly to each other. I sit down and kiss Garth on the cheek. "What's up?"

Ernestine rubs her hands together. "Your dad is talking to Henry right now. We're trying to decide if we should stay in the bunker tonight, just in case."

"What do you think, Ernestine?"

She shrugs. "I watched Henry bury someone on the hill today. I couldn't tell how sad he was about it. I think we better be on the safe side and stay in the bunker."

I nod as I realize how bad this rather rushed decision could turn out. "You're right. If he turns us in, we'll end up in the same situation as Avra."

Garth squeezes my knee with his deformed hand. "I think Henry'll understand. He recognizes his own value despite his heart problem. Don't give up hope this early."

Ding dong. That is the upstairs doorbell. "Get in the

bunker now!" Ernestine says as we gather up any evidence of our presence and hide behind the bookshelf.

I should be used to this by now, but I still hate it. There might be someone here ready to haul me back to the complex for all I know.

My mother is talking to someone as she descends the stairs. "As you can see, we have changed the color of this room from tan to burgundy."

A deep voice asks, "How is your escaped daughter's room coming along?"

"Don't call it that. It is the second guest room now. Elira is as good as dead, I'm sure. Haven't you caught her? I heard you caught most of the escapees."

The deep voice answers, "We caught two, but not her."

Mother's laugh is fake to my ears. "You'll figure it out. I don't know about you, but the election is taking all of my time these days. It's hard to think about anything else."

"Your son's chances are good. You should be proud."

"I am. Let's take a peek at how the second guest room is coming along before we have some strawberry-rhubarb pie a la mode."

I hear the stairs creak as Mother and the officer ascend the staircase again. I realize my whole body is tense. I force it to relax. Garth takes my hand and leads me to the couch. I melt into his side as he plays with my short blonde hair. "Your mother knows how to handle that peace officer. Just relax. Your dad should be home within the hour."

I lean my head against Garth's jaw. "Will his news be good or bad?"

Garth's breath tickles my ear as he whispers, "Good. We have to believe that people are naturally good at heart."

"Why?"

"If people aren't naturally good, then what are we fighting for?"

Click. The door swings open. My mom walks in with a pie and a stack of plates. "May I join you until Ross gets home?"

Garth jumps to his feet, takes the plates, and starts handing them out. "Yeah. But only because you brought us pie."

Mother smirks as she sets the pie on one of the beds. "I want to stay in here to understand how you must feel waiting for someone to let you out."

I love my mom for wanting to understand us. "It could be worse, Mom. Don't worry about us." She sits next to me on the couch. "I heard that peace officer talking about Brock's chances in the election. Do you think he could cause problems for Brock?"

Ernestine blurts out from one of the bottom bunks, "If he was going to do that, I think he would have done it already."

Mother nods. "I agree."

"Okay."

An hour later we're starting to doze off as the door opens

and Father walks in. I can't tell if he's happy or sad. He sees the plate of pie we left him on the closest bed, picks it up, and takes a big bite. I can't believe he would leave me in this much suspense. Garth and I stand up and stare at Father as he chews. "Well? Will Henry do it?" I ask.

Dad swallows and smiles. "Yes. He will do it, and it didn't even take a bribe."

Chapter 5

"WHICH CAR DO YOU WANT TO TAKE, Elira?"
my mom asks as my parents and I approach the garage the day
of the fair.

"Mine," I say enthusiastically.

"I thought you'd say that." Mother walks to the passenger
side of my purple car and stops before opening the door. "Wait.
Why is there a scratch on this door?"

"You'll have to ask the cactus that did it," I say as I slip into
the back seat.

"Oh," Mother says as she frowns at me.

Father gives me a sympathetic look as he climbs into

the driver's seat. "It was her first time driving. She did fine, Florence. I'm sure Bo at Car Essentials can make that scratch disappear in no time."

"Mmmhmm," Mother mutters through pursed lips.

I think it's a good time to change the subject. "Is Greggory going to meet us at the fair?"

Father nods his head. "Yes. He went early to ride a few rides first."

I keep twisting the ring on my finger around and around. "Oh, good. I won't be as nervous with him next to me."

As we pull into an enormous, crowded parking lot, I worry that my dad will run over people's feet as they swarm around our car, but surprisingly, no one cringes in pain. "Mom, are you sure they won't recognize me?"

Mother looks into the mirror on the sun visor to touch up her lipstick. "Yes, this crowding is your cover. If you don't recognize them, they won't recognize you."

"Okay." My hands refuse to work as I attempt to open the car door. I try to look at ease and confident as I join the throng of people heading to the entrance of the fairgrounds. This crowd is different than the crowd at the Vote-Off. There are so many people my age with brightly colored outfits and weird-looking haircuts. I don't know if what I'm feeling about them is intrigue or repulsion.

Mother and Father must not be as confused and lost as I am, because they walk us straight to a red colored booth with

'Brock Hamble for Senate' in white lettering. I see that Greggory beat us here. He yells out, "Edith is at the fair! I never thought I'd see the day."

A smiley middle-aged man greets us and brings us under the red canopy. "Doctor and Mrs. Hamble, thank you for volunteering tonight. This must be your niece, Edith." He sticks out his hand and smiles at me as I shake it. "I am Douglas Shriner."

"It's nice to meet you," I say through jittery lips.

Douglas doesn't seem to notice my nervousness. "Are you excited to be helping your cousin?" he asks with a smile.

"Y-yes," I say as I wobble in place.

"Excellent. We have two booths at the fair this year, one on each side of the fairgrounds. I'll need two of you to stay at this one and two of you to join my campaign vice president, Damon, at the other booth."

A middle-aged couple takes off the red 'Vote for Hamble' jackets they're wearing and hand them to my parents. "You must be our replacements. Put these on and we'll teach you how to approach people to give them a pamphlet." Mother and Father shrug at us and follow the couple.

Greggory looks at me and says, "I guess Edith and I will go to the other booth." Douglas smiles and claps us on the back. "That's the spirit. Walk directly east and look for a red canopy just like this. Damon will tell you what to do when you get there."

My parents smile encouragingly back at me as I follow Greggory through the crowds of people. Mother calls out, "Meet us back here when the fair shuts down for the night, you two."

"Okay," I call back.

Greggory is going faster than I am and I lose sight of him for a minute. I feel panic set in as a creepy-looking man with wild eyes smiles at me. I swear he bumps into me on purpose. "Hey, pretty girl, do you want to squeeze into a Ferris wheel seat with me?" I think the horror on my face scares the man off because he disappears as quickly as he came. Luckily, I see Greggory's messy blonde hair emerging from a group of people.

I run to him and grab his arm. "Greggory, I almost lost you. Will you hold my hand?"

Greggory looks at me like I'm the most pathetic child on earth. "Fine. You've got to get out more."

"I know."

A big red canopy materializes ahead of us. I'm relieved to hide under it for a few minutes and calm my pounding heart. Greggory drops my hand as a youngish man about Greggory's age with curly dark-brown hair and deep-blue eyes greets us under the shade of the canopy. He has a pleasant smile. "Hello. I'm Damon Bellvue, the vice president of the Herrington Brock Hamble for Senate campaign."

My brother shakes Damon's hand. "Yeah. I'm Greggory Hamble. Here to help my brother out. This is my cousin, Edith."

Damon's eyes stay on my face for longer than is comfortable. Is he looking at the raised skin of my raccoon eye? Does he recognize me? "Hello, Edith. You look so familiar. Have we met before?"

I start twisting my ring around again. "No. I don't think so. I live in Trenton. I am visiting my aunt and uncle."

"Do you mind my asking how old you are?"

Greggory's eyes widen as I look to him for help. "I-I'm s…" Greggory shakes his head at me. "Eighteen."

"So you're newly out on your own and already excited to play a part in politics? I like that," Damon says appreciatively.

"Uh, yeah."

Damon's eyes stay on me as he calls out, "Rebecca and Vince, your replacements are here. You're free to go. Please leave your jackets with Greggory and Edith." I wish Damon would look away. Rebecca seems relieved to go. She throws me her jacket and rushes off.

Vince hands his jacket to Greggory carefully and respectfully. "I am honored to meet the brother of Brock Hamble." He takes Greggory's hand and shakes it firmly. "Brock is the greatest man I have ever known, and if there is anything else I can do to get him elected, please let me know." He takes two cards out of his wallet and hands one to Damon and the other one to Greggory.

Greggory looks perplexed as he watches Vince leave.

"I'm going to hang on to this card. I'm sure I can come up with something for him to do."

"Greggory, you're terrible," I say as I shake my head.

Damon watches us thoughtfully. "You aren't a believer in Brock's goodness?"

Greggory shrugs. "I don't know. I guess so. He's not the most perfect brother in the world though."

"That's understandable. What brother is? Let me show you how I make an approach then the two of you will stand on opposite corners of the canopy and convince people to take brochures and buttons and ultimately vote for Brock."

It isn't as hard as I expected. I believe in the things that Brock represents so I don't have a hard time declaring the virtues of my brother. I don't talk about The Complex Law until three pregnant women approach me. Two of them are happy and enjoying the fair. One of them is trying not to show the misery that is evident in her eyes.

The pregnant, spikey-haired blonde approaches me first. I recognize her from the Herrington Vote-Off. Luckily, she doesn't recognize me as the belly-toucher without my red, curly wig. She eyes me seriously. "What is Brock Hamble's stance on The Complex Law?"

Greggory shoots me a pointed look and shakes his head. I have to say something though. "This pamphlet declares that he's neutral toward it, but I happen to know, as his cousin, that he is personally against it."

The blonde smiles. "See, Molly? I knew he was anti-complex. Take a pamphlet and vote for him."

"That says he's neutral," Molly wails as she tugs on a strand of her curly brown hair.

"Are you anti-complex, Molly?" I ask.

The somber woman looks at me with puffy eyes. "I was neutral until a month ago. Now that I know my baby has whatever-it-is syndrome, I don't want all of this hard work to be for nothing."

The third pregnant woman with short black hair leans toward me. "We three have been best friends since high school. We decided three years ago to plan our pregnancies together for this year. We were going to watch our babies grow up together, but now Molly won't be able to keep hers."

Anger burns through my veins; I need to be careful about what I say. I reach out and pat Molly's arm. "That's terrible and wrong." Molly nods and wipes her nose on her hand.

The spikey-haired blonde shrugs her shoulders. "Yeah, I guess."

I feel anger rising like a flood in me. "No. Not I guess. It is wrong. We can't let the government do this to Molly and her precious baby. Vote for Brock and write letters to President Prystine telling him that the Complex Law is outdated and needs to be repealed."

Molly wipes her eyes with a wadded-up tissue. "People get in trouble when they do stuff like that."

"Times are changing, Molly. Can I get your phone number and address, so I can contact you with more information later?"

"Sure." Molly writes her contact information on a piece of paper for me.

I try to avoid Greggory's warning eyes as I whisper into her ear. "Do you want your baby to have the chance to learn and grow by your side?

She whispers through her tears, "Yes, more than anything."

I slap the stack of pamphlets I'm holding against my leg. "Your children will thank you for standing up for their rights. You must do what you can for them."

The blonde and the other friend look at me hesitantly, but Molly takes a pamphlet from me and holds it up like a banner. "I'm going to tell the man running for mayor of Herrington how I feel right now. Come on, girls."

I watch as Molly and her friends march to the blue canopy that says 'Johnathan Lawrence for Mayor' and basically start a riot. I watch carefully to see if the people watching agree with Molly or not. I have to say, at least half of them seem to be nodding along with her.

Damon sidles up next to me. "Nice work there, Edith. You know how to move people to action. Not many people care to make a difference these days. They just do what has always been done or what the loudest voice in their lives tells them to do."

Greggory shakes his head at me. "The loudest voice in

this country is the government, and drawing attention to our discontent can cause us problems, if you know what I mean."

He's right; I should've kept my mouth shut. I apologize to both guys. "I'm sorry. I know Brock doesn't want to look anti-complex until he is elected."

Damon straightens his stack of pamphlets. "I—I didn't know he was anti-complex. It doesn't surprise me too much though."

I try not to show my surprise. "Why? Because of his sister?"

Damon's eyes look at me curiously. "No. It just feels like the masses are shifting that direction. You know about his sister?"

I shrug my shoulders and smile. "Of course I do. They are my cousins."

"We are trying to keep that information under wraps until the election is over."

I feel my anger rising again. "Brock is anti-complex because taking people away from their families to work for no pay is wrong." I turn my back on Damon and march under the canopy to grab a bottle of water out of the 'Brock for Senate' cooler.

Greggory glares at me then turns to Damon and smiles. "Sorry about my cousin. She has her hot button topics. She's actually a..."

"Firecracker. I like her," Damon smiles at me and leaves to get a hamburger.

I lose count of how many pamphlets I hand out after I reach 500. I only prick my finger once pinning a 'Brock Hamble for Senate' pin on a pimply teenage girl.

Damon wanders back to us after half an hour and hands me a big scone covered in strawberries and cream. "Are you hungry, Edith?"

My mouth waters as the aroma of the heavenly confection he's carrying wafts toward me. "I am if you're offering this."

Damon smiles as he leaves it in my hands. "I had a feeling you'd like it."

"Did you bring me one?" Greggory asks.

Damon backpedals. "Oh, I..."

"I'll share it with you, Greggory."

Damon rubs his hand through his curly, dark hair. "You two sit down and eat for a few minutes. I'll cover for you."

Greggory watches Damon closely as he fills his jacket pockets with pins and grabs a stack of pamphlets. "Elira, I think he likes you," Greggory whispers as he cuts the scone thing in half.

I sigh as I take a bite. "Whatever. He just likes to see people my age politically active."

My brother narrows his eyes. "No. He might have bought a soda for someone he admires that way. For you he bought a funnel cake with strawberries and cream."

I take another bite. "You are just a paranoid older brother."

Greggory shoves an abnormally large bite into his mouth and says while he chews, "I've lived in this world longer than you have. I know I'm right."

The strawberries that were sweet in my mouth suddenly turn sour. "You can finish my half. I'm getting back to work." I wipe my hands on a napkin then pick up a stack of pamphlets.

I'm sure I convince at least ten people who were not planning to vote for Brock to change their minds. Damon smiles at me and nods every time I succeed. It makes me blush and feel weird when he does. When half of the lights go out and people start moving as a mass to the exits, I know the fair is shutting down and that I can go home and rest my tired feet. I take off the red jacket and lay it on the table under the canopy.

Damon walks toward me with a metal button in his hand. "Can I pin a button on each of you before you leave?"

I shrug. "Sure." Damon sticks his finger through the neck of my shirt to keep from pricking me with the back of the pin. I feel my breath catch in my throat. When I'm this close to him, I notice that he has some tiny little freckles that I didn't notice before. Damon takes his time making sure the pin is straight. I haven't worn a pin since I left the complex. I can't remember how long ago that was exactly. I can't think clearly for some reason.

A familiar voice says, "Edith! Imagine meeting you here."

Garth appears before Damon and me with his parents and brother.

I feel my cheeks turn red. "H-hi, G-Garrett. What are you doing here?"

"Joseph wanted to go on the rides for his birthday."

I force a smile on my face. "Oh, of course. Greggory and I were just leaving to go home."

Garth pushes my hair behind my ear. "We'll walk you part of the way."

"Okay." I turn around and wave. "Goodbye, Damon. I'm sure I'll see you again before the election."

Damon's eyes grab a hold of mine. "I look forward to it. Goodbye, Edith." I force my eyes to look away.

Garth's cute little brother, Joseph, is as happy and energetic as ever. "Hey! It's my birthday. Guess how old I am."

I pretend to be baffled. "Uh, seven?"

Joseph's nose crinkles. "Are you kidding me? I'm ten!"

I smile and rub my hand over his short, dirty-blonde hair. "Oh, of course, you are."

Joseph bumps Garth with his elbow. "Gar-Garrett said we couldn't leave until we found you."

"Really? It's a good thing you found me then, or you'd be here all night." Joseph laughs. I fall into step with Garth and mutter under my breath, "So, Garrett, this is a bit of a risk."

Garth grins apologetically. "I know. I just wanted a kiss." He leans over and plants a kiss right on my lips. When he pulls away, I look behind us and see Damon glaring at us as he stacks the remaining pamphlets on the table.

Greggory comes around my other side and whispers in my ear, "I told you he liked you." I punch him in the arm and glare at him as we make our way to my parents' booth.

I feel Garth press something into my hand. "I bought you something."

I look in my hand to find a keychain shaped like a purple rose. "It's beautiful. I thought you said you were going to make me a keychain."

"I know. I started carving a rose like this, the way Rocky's dad taught me to, but I accidently broke it yesterday. When I saw this one at a booth today, I had to buy it for you."

"I love it. I can't wait to put my key on it."

Garth's parents are quiet today. I hope the news about Jefrey doesn't have them upset at each other. They aren't very peppy when I introduce them to Greggory. They start moving to the right and his mom says, "We're parked this way, boys. So long, El-Edith and Greggory."

I wave sweetly. "It was nice to see you again. Goodbye."

"I'll see you later," Garth says as he kisses me again and leaves with his family. I smile silently at him as he leaves.

Greggory pulls me along to the other big red canopy. "You are a heartbreaker, little sister."

"Shut up," I say as I try to wrap my head around what Greggory is hinting at.

My parents take off their red jackets and join us as we walk to the parking lot. My mom puts her arm around me. "Did you learn anything interesting tonight?"

I'm walking forward but my mind is reeling backward. "Yes, Mom. I sure did."

Chapter 6

I LOVE THE FEEL OF THE GRASS beneath my hands as I close my eyes and stretch out on the back lawn we just mowed and weeded for my mom. It smells so fresh and alive out here. The sun falls on my face with warm tendrils of light. My usually dark eyelids can't keep the brightness out, which is surprisingly okay with me. Someday soon I'll have Avra and Shasta lie on the grass with me too. They will love this sensation. I feel something fuzzy tickling my nose, so I open my eyes. A fluffy white cat is staring at me from Garth's outstretched hands. His tail keeps tickling my face.

"Look what I caught."

I smile and sit up. "I've seen him out the window. I love him."

"I knew you would. Do you want to hold him?"

"Yes!" I relish the softness of the cat's fluffy fur as he cuddles up in my lap. "Whose is he?"

Garth shrugs as he teases the cat with one of the weeds we've been pulling today. I think it's called a dandelion. "I don't know, but he's tame, and he hangs out in the yard a lot. I think Freda feeds him her food scraps."

I startle as the cat starts pulsating like a car motor in my arms. "What's wrong with him?"

Garth laughs at me. "I think it's called purring. He likes you. I think you should name him."

"If I name him, I'll probably cry when his owner takes him away one of these days."

Garth is in a teasing mood. "Well, if you don't name him, I'll name him—Alexander Prystine."

"Ick!" I throw a fistful of grass at him. "That gives me an idea though; I will name him—President."

Garth laughs. "Ha! I like it. Do you like it, Mr. President?" I take his purring as a yes.

Damp green stuff suddenly falls from the sky onto our heads. I cover President with my arms to protect him from it. Garth swings around. "What the—Rocky!"

Our friend bursts out laughing as he watches us pull grass

and weeds off our heads. "You two seemed way too comfortable for your own good."

President loses patience with us, jumps out of my lap, and runs away. "Rocky! You scared the cat away. Get him, Garth."

Garth jumps up and starts running after the cat.

"No! Not the cat; get Rocky!" I laugh. Rocky's smile turns to dread as Garth takes off after him.

Garth tackles his skinnier friend to the ground and gives him a handful of grass to eat. Rocky barely has enough air to say, "No! Get off, you ape!"

A deep voice clears his throat. "Hey, you three. I wondered if you wanted to have another driving lesson today, but if you'd rather play in the grass..." My dad taps his foot as he looks at the three of us on the ground.

Garth immediately jumps to his feet and brushes himself off. "No! We want to drive, Mr. Hamble. We'll have this mess cleaned up in half a minute."

"Good. Meet me at Elira's car in five."

I laugh as I watch Rocky's green-stained face concentrating as he rakes up the armful of weeds he dumped on our heads. Garth and I help him haul them to the pile behind the shop.

As my dad drives us out of town and into the desert, I rest my head on Garth's shoulder. Rocky turns around from the front passenger seat and asks, "Can I drive first this time?"

I shrug. "Sure, why?"

"I don't want you to kill me before I get my turn."

"If I could reach you, Rocky Moore…"

"You couldn't get me if you tried."

Garth snickers at his friend. "Hey, Rocky, you got a little something right there," he says as he points to a spot next to his own mouth." Rocky pulls the sun visor mirror down and scowls as he wipes at the green streak off his cheek.

My dad stops the car and puts a hand on Rocky's shoulder. "Hey, you three, quit acting like brothers and sisters. We're here. Are you going first, Rocky?"

"Yep."

I relax and enjoy my Garth pillow as Rocky drives us around for a while. Garth is everything that makes me happy. Damon couldn't make me feel this way, could he? "What is your favorite thing about today?" I ask my boyfriend.

Garth plays with the hair on my forehead. "Having you this close."

"I thought you'd say driving."

He sighs. "It's a close number two."

I lose my comfortable pillow sooner than I'd like. "Elira, it's your turn," my dad says.

I reluctantly leave Garth's side and climb into the driver's seat. "What should I do, Dad?"

He points ahead of us. "Go around the obstacle course and then park next to that rusty old silo down there."

"Okay." I think I'm doing better than last time as I make my turns. I don't nick any cones or cacti at least.

When I park next to the silo, my dad turns to me. "I want you to back up, flip around, and park with your tail end first."

"Uh, okay." I back up and flip around okay, but when I'm backing into the made-up parking space, I accidently bump the silo and the old metal rips open.

"Elira! Pull forward," my dad says angrily. I obey him without looking into anyone's eyes.

Someone is snickering behind me. I turn around when Rocky busts out laughing. "I knew I should go first, before you totaled the car."

I don't appreciate his exaggeration. "I didn't total the car! I bet it didn't even hurt the car."

"Let's get out and see," my dad says unenthusiastically.

I am right about one thing; it didn't do more than scratch the bumper of my car. At least it will match the scratch on the passenger-side door. Unfortunately, the silo now has a huge flap of metal scraped to the side, which leaves a gaping hole in the side of it.

My dad scratches his chin. "I'll just bend that back in place, but I'll still have to give Elmer some money to fix it."

Rocky shakes his head as he peers into the hole. "This whole thing is a big rust can. All of the metal needs replaced, or maybe it should be torn down."

I feel like such an idiot. "Dad, I'm so sorry."

He waves it off like it's nothing. "It's okay." My dad walks over to the bent, splintering flap and uses both hands to tug on the rusty metal to bend it back. He pulls so hard that he kind of loses his balance and slips or stumbles or something. When he rights himself, the remaining rusty metal is barely hanging on to the building by a thread and both of his hands are bleeding.

"Dad!" I scream as try to reach him. For some reason, I stop and sink to the ground. That much blood kind of makes my stomach feel funny.

Garth pulls me up and takes me to the car to sit down.

"Garth, what do we have to wrap his hands with?" Rocky asks as he looks around. We don't really have anything except cones and cardboard boxes out here.

My father's voice is shaky as he says, "We usually keep a blanket in the trunk of the car. Will you boys wrap my hands for me?"

"Yes, Mr. Hamble," Rocky says as he opens the trunk. "Uh, what else do we have? There isn't a blanket in here."

My father sighs. "I guess Florence hasn't put one in Elira's car yet. If you can get me to my office, I have everything I need there."

"Yes. I will get you there. Mr. Hamble," Garth says as he takes off his shirt and rips it in half. He hands Rocky one half of the shirt as he wraps one of my father's hands in the other half.

I feel my breath catch in my throat as I notice that Garth has bigger muscles than I had imagined, or maybe it's just shock at my dad's predicament... Either way, Garth's white undershirt thing doesn't hide much of him... He doesn't notice my gaping jaw as he helps my dad get in the passenger seat of my car. Once he has my dad settled, he gets behind the wheel and tells us to buckle up. Why was I thinking about Damon, again?

"I can drive if you want, Garth," Rocky says.

My handsome boyfriend shakes his head. "No. I'll do it. You calm Elira down. I know how to get back to Herrington. I'll just need you to guide me from there, Mr. Hamble. How are you feeling?"

"Okay, but I think I can feel myself going into shock."

Garth's voice is steady and confident. "I'll get you to your office as quickly as I can."

"Thank you."

I put a hand on Garth's bare shoulder. "Don't speed once we get to Herrington; peace officers will pull you over for sure."

"I'll slow down once we get there." Garth steps on the gas and we fly down the dirt road to the main highway. I keep looking from my father, who has turned white, to my boyfriend, who has literally given him the shirt off his back and is driving without much experience to a city that doesn't accept people like us. What a crazy afternoon this is turning out to be.

Rocky looks at me curiously. "You don't look so good. Lie back and put your feet on me. Mr. Hamble, you do the same thing. Lower your head and raise your feet."

"You're right, young man. How did you know how to treat shock?"

"My dad told me after I accidently knocked something heavy on both of his feet."

"That's a terrible way to learn about it."

"Yeah." Rocky is suddenly getting squished by my dad's reclining seat and my feet. He doesn't complain. Rocky is a tease, but when there is trouble, he knows what matters.

"Okay, Mr. Hamble. Where do I go from here?" Garth asks as we enter the city.

My dad mumbles a little bit, but none of us can understand what he is saying.

Garth raises his voice to snap my dad out of his stupor. "Ross! I need to know which way to go!"

My father's voice becomes understandable. "Go straight until you get to Medical Parkway, then turn right. Look for my name on the sign."

I'm not sure if that is enough to go on. I hope we don't get lost. Maybe we should go home instead. "Do you think you can get us there, Garth?"

"Yes. I remember passing Medical Parkway on the way in. There was a building shaped like an ice cream cone on the corner."

I'm surprised to see that he's right. There is a huge ice cream cone shaped building on the corner where we turn. The sign reads, 'Double Scoop It.' Garth drives slowly down the road filled with medical buildings and pulls into the one that says, 'Herrington Cardiology Center.'

I look frantically around, afraid we're in the wrong place. "Garth, I don't see his name."

Garth points up. "It's right there, under the big words."

My brain finally clicks into place. "Oh, yeah. I'm so glad you are here. It looks like everyone has gone home for the night."

He opens my door and holds my hands, which I realize are surprisingly cold. He leans in to kiss me before he asks, "Are you able to walk?"

"Yes. Help my Dad." He kisses me one more time before walking to the other side of the car to help Rocky lead my dad to the door."

"Garth, the biggest key on my keyring will open the door."

Garth opens the door and we follow my father's instructions to the back of the building. I have to sit down again when we unwrap Dad's hands. The rusty metal must have fallen apart into a hundred little knife-like shards that embedded themselves into my father's hands. Rocky and Garth take tweezers and pull each of the little metal slivers out of his palms while I sit there helplessly.

Watching my dad cringe makes me sad. "Are you okay, Dad?"

He forces a smile for me. "Yes. This will be fine. None of these are deep. It's a lot of blood without a lot of bite."

I remember something important. "Will you be able to do

your presentation and heart murmur checks tomorrow?" I ask as worry fills my mind for someone else in trouble.

"Yes. I'll just bandage my hands and wear plastic gloves like I usually do. I've had a tetanus shot recently. It will be fine, my love."

"I'm so sorry."

"Don't keep saying that. It's fine. I'll be a new person tomorrow. In fact, look, all the shards are gone." My dad points to a tall clear bottle on the counter. "Take that disinfectant over there and clean my hands off. I'll be almost as good as new." I still don't feel so good. I lay down on the row of chairs I'm sitting on.

Garth takes the liquid and dumps it on his hands. My father flinches, but his hands do look much better once they are cleaned off. Garth and Rocky wrap his hands in gauze and bandages, and he smiles as they clean up the mess. He extends his hands towards me. "See, Elira. All better."

I wrap my arms around him and kiss his cheek. "Maybe everyone would be safer if I give up on driving."

"No. You'll get it. No one is perfect at something new. Well, Garth is getting there awfully fast. Would you be willing to drive us back home, Garth?"

"I'd love to. Thank you."

"No, thank you."

Chapter 7

FRIDAY IS FINALLY HERE. If everything goes to plan, we are going to rescue Avra today! Mother handed off the sheol to Maxine without a problem; she liked my mother's idea to take her five-year-old troublemaker to isolation today. I decide to eat breakfast with my dad upstairs before he leaves for the complex. I don't know if I expect this to calm my nerves or what, but it's not working.

My hand shakes each time I raise a bite of omelet to my mouth. "Dad, how are your hands?"

He sets his fork down and looks at them. He smiles like his

life is perfect. "Much better. See? Only four bandages per hand today. Once I have gloves on, no one will ever know."

My lower lip quivers as I imagine what he is about to do. "I wish I could help you in the complex today."

He sighs. "I know, Elira. I wish you could personally remove Avra from that building, too, but I won't risk losing you again. You'll just have to trust us oldie moldies to do it."

I grin at my dad. "You're not moldy."

"Tell that to your brothers."

I giggle and then become serious. "Ernestine says she'll drive me to the hill to watch. Across the street, anyway."

"I would wear a different disguise, both of you. What if someone asks you what you're doing?"

"I'm going to take a big map and say we're lost."

Dad wipes his mouth with a napkin and stands up. "That should work."

I wrap my arms around him. "Dad, I'm so afraid that she's already dead, or that she won't wake up from the sheol. Please, bring her back here, safe and sound."

My dad has more confidence than I do. "I will, honey."

His bandaged hands fold gently over my own. My mind switches from Avra laying lifeless on a bed to my gentle dad lying to the complex doctors. "Be careful. I don't want to lose you too."

He waves off my fears. "I'll be fine. I'll see you back here at 4:00—you and Avra."

A smile erupts onto my face. "I can't wait to see her again! I love you, Dad."

"I love you, too." Dad kisses my forehead and leaves for the complex with a grim look on his face.

"ERNESTINE, DON'T PARK TOO CLOSE to the road."

"I can't get off any farther. This is fine."

I fiddle with the long, black wig I'm wearing. "Where will they send her body out of the building?"

Ernestine points to the complex. "When I spent all those nights snooping around this place, they usually sent the body bags out that side door by the skinny driveway. A covered black truck would pull up to the door and the body bag was placed inside."

"When will Henry switch Avra for the bag of rocks?"

"I'm sure he has the body bag of rocks ready in the back of his truck."

Movement in that area makes me gasp. I can't believe we're doing this. "Look! Here comes the truck!"

Ernestine pulls something I've never seen before out of her giant purse thing. "I only have one pair of binoculars. They make things seem closer when you hold them to your eyes. Do you want to keep watch for us?"

I snatch them out of Ernestine's hand. "Yes. Thank you."

I am amazed at how close the complex side door is when I look through the binoculars. The black truck isn't all black, I notice, as it backs up next to the complex side door. The words 'Herrington Complex Undertaker' in white letters adorn the back hatch.

I start breathing faster. "What if this doesn't work, Ernestine? What if she doesn't wake up? What if Dad gets caught lying?"

Ernestine slips a finger under her blonde wig to scratch her head. "They won't do anything to him. They'll just think it was an honest mistake, that he thought she was dead. Avra, on the other hand, I don't know what they will do to her. Probably finish her off."

I gulp. That was not what I wanted to hear; this could all go very wrong. Through the binoculars, I see a burly middle-aged man with a scruffy salt-and-pepper beard get out of the black undertaker truck and knock on the complex door. That must be my dad's friend, Henry Ricks. As I press the binoculars harder into my face, I see the door knobturn and someone, Doctor James, it looks like, walking backwards out of it. He is holding onto handles at the end of a big black bag. Henry opens the back of his truck and takes the end of the black bag away from Doctor James. My heart starts beating faster as I recognize the man holding the other end of the bag. My father, with plastic gloves on his hands, helps Henry hoist the body bag into the truck. I shudder as I watch his poor hands. I hope they are being careful with Avra. What if she can't breathe in there?

Ernestine pulls the binoculars away from me and takes a look. "I can't believe it. This might actually work."

I grab them back. "What if Doctor James sees the other body bag in the truck?"

Ernestine scratches under her wig again. "Is he poking around in there?"

My pulse quickens. "Not really, but I swear he's looking right at something big and black in the truck."

"Shut the doors to the truck, Ross," Ernestine pleads aloud.

I see Henry clap Doctor James on the shoulder and inconspicuously turn him away from the truck as he tells him something funny. My dad shuts the doors on the back of the truck and shakes both men's hands. I'm sure the handshakes are painful, but he doesn't show it on his face. My dad then leads Doctor James back to the door of the complex, and after his colleague unlocks it, they go inside. Henry gets into the front of his truck and drives away.

I might jump out of my skin. "Let's go, Ernestine! She can't breathe in there."

Ernestine turns on the car and makes a U-turn on the road. "I just hope there is breath left in her," she mutters.

Chapter 8

WE STAY ON THE MAIN ROAD as we watch the big black truck maneuver the small road that connects The Complex of Undesirables to the burial hill and The Complex for the Elderly. We stop just past the hill and pull over again. I put the binoculars to my face with anxiety. "I think he just unzipped the body bag a little bit. I hope she had enough air in there."

Ernestine leans over the steering wheel to get a better view of the black truck. "The sheol causes her breathing to become so shallow, she probably had enough air for that short amount of time."

"I hope so," I say as I watch Henry join another man who is

already digging a hole near the truck. I see the sweat glistening off their foreheads as they work. It's taking longer than I thought it would. How deep does the hole have to be?

"Oh no," Ernestine mutters as we see flashing lights approaching us from behind.

I stuff the binoculars inside the bag. "What's going on, Ernestine?"

"Peace officers are right behind us. When they come to my window, remember your fake name and that we are lost. Unfold the map as big as it goes. Now."

I obediently unfold the map to its maximum size and will my hands to stop shaking as I hold it to my face. A young, blonde peace officer approaches Ernestine's window. She rolls it down.

"Excuse me, ma'am, are you aware that this is a no parking zone?"

Ernestine smiles at the officer. "I'm so sorry, we are lost. We're trying to get to the Herrington Museum."

"Your license plates say you're from Herrington. How could you come this far past the city and not know to turn back?"

Ernestine pauses for a second. "We don't get out much and we're terrible with directions. Can you help us?" She asks.

The peace officer frowns. "I don't have time to be escorting lost females all over the countryside."

I lower my map and lean toward him. "Isn't it just

straight for a few miles and then we turn left at the second intersection?"

The officer leans closer to the window and looks at me. I feel my heart start to pound. Does he recognize me? I feel his eyes memorizing every detail of my face. "I'm sorry. I should be more help to respectable citizens like yourselves. I'll lead you right to the museum. I could even show you where the best exhibit is, if you want a tour guide."

I'm thrown off by the change in the officer's attitude. "I-uh, thank you. We'll follow you back into town, but we want to spend more time than you can spare in the museum, so a tour won't be necessary."

"Okay. Just follow me, ladies."

Ernestine rolls up her window as the officer walks back to his car. I follow his progress with my eyes out of curiosity. "What is his issue?"

Ernestine snorts. "He thinks you're pretty."

The officer smiles and waves as he pulls in front of us. I huff, "We'll have to follow him now. Dang. I want to see Avra as soon as possible." As I turn to look at the hill, Henry is lowering a big black bag into the hole they just dug. I wonder if his helper can tell if it's a bag of rocks. He's leaning against the side of the black truck making smoke with something in his mouth, so hopefully he's too preoccupied to notice.

Ernestine is breathing fast. "We can still make this work, Elira. When we get to the museum, we'll have to stay there and look around for at least an hour. I'll call Florence from inside the museum and have her and Scott meet Henry at the hand-off place to get Avra."

"Where is the hand-off place again?"

"The sporting goods store. A long black bag could be holding bats, or nets, or something else sporty, so we won't look suspicious."

"Okay," I say glumly.

"Cheer up, kid. Your friend is out of the complex!"

I continue to frown. "I wish I could be the first one to see her, but we have to lose this officer, or we're sunk."

We drive in silence as we follow the young peace officer to the museum. Once we park, he rushes to my side of the car and opens the door for me. Ernestine grins as he smiles and walks with us to the entrance of the museum. I am losing my patience. "Thank you, officer, for helping us find our way. I have hours of boring research to do in here, so I better get to it. Please look out for yourself as you keep our city safe."

The blonde peace officer smiles at me. "I will. Safety is my motto. Say, do you want to grab a bite to eat later tonight?"

You've got to be kidding me. "I'm afraid I can't. My boyfriend and I have plans tonight, but thank you for the offer."

The peace officer's smile melts off his face. "You ladies have a nice day," he says as he trudges back to his car.

I call out to his retreating back loudly. "We will. Thank you."

Ernestine chuckles as we enter the museum. "Maybe you should make your disguises a little bit uglier."

"It's not funny."

Ernestine pats my back. "You're right. You actually saved us back there."

We pay our admission and pretend to be interested in the History of Herrington displays on the first floor. I learn that mayors of Herrington serve for eight years and can be reelected once. I would normally be thrilled to absorb this information in order to understand my new world better, but all I can think about is Avra in a body bag not far from here. Ernestine uses the receptionist's phone to call my mother. I'm sure Ernestine's creative code words are hilarious to overhear but I can't hear her from here.

I peek out every window I come across until I get a good view of the parking lot. "He's gone, Ernestine. Let's go."

She looks at her watch. "It's been 45 minutes. He might still be in the area. We'll wait 15 more minutes, then we'll go."

I groan and force myself to read a big display that explains how the government works in this country. It's actually helpful to learn that each city in The United Cities has one senator to represent it on a national level. The office lasts for 10 years, and a person can only be reelected once. Every citizen in the country gets to vote on all senators, not just the one from their city. Presidential candidates must be at least 38 years old, and if elected, will hold the office until death or when they reach the age of 80 which requires them to retire to a Complex for the Elderly.

An elderly, male museum worker approaches us. "I don't know if you noticed when you paid for your admission, but the museum closes an hour earlier than usual on Fridays. Make sure you use your time wisely."

Ernestine smiles at the man. "Thank you for the reminder. We were just about to leave anyway."

My heart skips a beat as the man walks away. I whisper excitedly, "Can we go see Avra now?"

Ernestine smirks at me and shakes her head. "Actually, if we wait until closing time—Just kidding! Let's go."

I think my body is the only thing that is keeping my insides from exploding with anticipation. There's a little bit of guilt thrown in there, too. I wish I had kept my best friend from being captured, but she is out of the complex now. I just hope she is strong enough to wake up from the effects of the sheol.

As soon as Ernestine parks the black car in the garage, I fly into the house. I am greeted by a somber-looking Garth in the basement great room.

"Where is she, Garth?"

My boyfriend places his hands on my arms. "We put her in the bunker on a bottom bunk, but she hasn't woken up yet. Your dad just got here, and he set her up on a thing called an IV to give her a boost of nutrition and fluids. He also gave her a shot of adrenaline to give her enough energy to wake up."

I don't care. I just want to see her. Why is he standing in my way? "Let me see her," I say as I try to pass him.

Garth doesn't let me get by him. He takes me by the hand and says, "She looks bad, Elira. Prepare yourself."

Chapter 9

I WASTE NO TIME GETTING TO THE DOOR of the hidden room. My mother and Scott are sitting on folding chairs next to the closest bunk bed. My best friend is lying in the bed looking completely lifeless. Her face is thin and sunken in. She has lost so much hair, her head is showing through it in an unhealthy way. Her arms and legs are skeletally thin and bruised. I push past my mom and sink to the floor by the bed.

I pick Avra's frail hand up and cringe when I feel no heat or life in it. I feel tears dripping off my cheeks before I even know they've formed. I lean close to her ear and say, "Avra, please wake up. I've missed you. I will never let anyone take you away again. Just please wake up."

My father clears his throat behind me. "It's 5:00. She should be at least twitching or breathing deeper by now. This isn't a good sign, honey."

I turn around and yell, "No! No, I won't accept that. Maybe Maxine gave the sheol to her later than noon."

Mother squeezes my shoulder. "Maxine called me on her lunch break. She said she took the troublemaker in her dorm to a private cell at 11:30 and volunteered to help give Avra her injection of medicine soon after that. She said she slipped the sheol into Avra's mouth at 11:55 on the dot."

I wipe my nose on the back of my hand. "Was she conscious when Maxine gave it to her?"

"No, darling, she wasn't conscious."

Father squeezes in next to us to check Avra's pulse. He frowns. "I can feel her pulse, but it's extremely faint. She looks exactly the same as when I declared her dead in the complex. That was at 2:00 exactly. Dr. James didn't even check her himself. He said he has been expecting her to go for several days now.

I feel my sadness transform into anger. "What can we do? I can't just sit here and watch her die, Dad."

"I have given her everything I know to help her come out of it. I will do some research. If I find anything else that might help, we'll try it."

Mother sighs as she lovingly pats my back. "I had a cat when I was a girl that I never gave much attention. It developed a disease, a cancer maybe, that started eating away the cat's nose. My parents took it to the veterinarian, but the vet said that there was nothing we could do. He could put the cat down or we could let the cat die at home. We decided to bring it home."

I grimace. "Mom, I don't want to hear this right now. I don't want Avra to die."

"Just listen. We brought the cat home and I decided that he would spend the last days of his life like a king. I made him a bed out of fluffy pillows, I fed him fresh tuna fish and cream from a dish, I brushed his fur and kept him clean and fluffy, I even put the same ointment that I put on my own cuts and scrapes on his nose. Guess what happened."

I frown at my mother. "He died comfortably."

Mother smiles at me. "No. His nose grew back. He lived."

I feel my eyebrows trying to touch each other. "How can that be?"

"Our health is affected by the way we're treated. When the cat didn't think anyone cared about his suffering, he was ready to die of his ailment. As soon as he knew I cared and wanted him to be comfortable, he had something to live for."

"So what's your point?"

"We may have given her all the medical attention we can give her, but we can still show her that we care for her and love her."

I lift the lifeless hand that I'm holding. "She doesn't even know I'm here."

"You don't know that. She might be listening to every word we say. Tell her how much you care about her. Go get your lotion. Rub it into her hands and feet. Paint her nails. She needs to know that we care and that she has something worth living for."

Chapter 10

"ELIRA, YOU'VE BEEN IN THIS DARK ROOM with Avra all night and all day. Why don't you come with me to the mall?" my mother pleads from beside the bunkbed.

My voice is hoarse and strained. "I don't remember what that is."

"It's a big building with lots of little stores inside. You can walk from store to store and get everything you need in one place."

I close my eyes and lay my head next to my friend on her pillow. "I don't want to shop. I want Avra to wake up."

"I know you do, darling. She was in such bad shape, she may need time for the fluids and nutrients we're giving her to work. Let's get away for a few hours. Brock will be at the mall today answering questions and taking pictures with voters. We could stop by and see him."

I look at Avra and see no change in her face or her ultra-shallow breathing. Maybe I should go outside and stretch my legs. "Can Garth come with me?"

"No. He and Rocky are going to help Rocky's dad paint the outside of his house today."

"Oh yeah."

"We haven't had a mother-daughter day since your birthday. Scott will stay with Avra, and we can get our nails done again."

My mother's begging face is hard to resist. "Okay, fine. Let's go."

I put on my Edith Westergard disguise and follow my mom to the garage. "Are you ready to try driving, Elira?"

I open the passenger side of my purple car and climb in. "No. According to Rocky, I may never be ready."

Mother climbs into the driver's side. "Don't be ridiculous. I'm sure you're closer than you know."

We sit in silence as we drive. I wish I had something happy or exciting to talk about, but I don't. "How many more days till the election?"

"What's today? Saturday, so three more days."

"Good. It's time to take that death factory down."

"Yes, it is." Mother gives my arm a squeeze. "Let's talk about something more upbeat. "Greggory is coming after he gets off work tonight and is staying the weekend with us. Won't that be fun?"

The corners of my mouth turn up a little bit. "Yeah, that will be fun."

"When I told him that we had Avra back, he insisted on coming to see her."

I give her half a smile. "I'm glad he's coming. He's always a good distraction."

When we get to the mall, Mother insists we get manicures first. "A new manicure always cheers me up. That's exactly what you need today, darling."

Our manicurists are chatty and sweet, and my pretty red nails do cheer me up a little bit. We start walking down the hall in the mall when we see a big group of people in the center court. I try to avoid eye contact with the people in the crowd and slip by them when I hear someone call out, "Edith! Edith, it's me, Damon Bellvue."

I turn around as Damon nabs my arm. "Hi, Damon. What are you doing here?"

"I'm helping Brock with his question-and-answer session. Didn't you know that? I figured that was why you're here."

"Oh, yeah. I did know that. I just didn't think this crowd

was his crowd. I'm actually here to shop with my m—aunt and get my mind off—things."

Damon's eyes see the pain in my own. "What things? Can I help?"

Mother clears her throat beside me. "Oh, Damon, I would like to introduce you to my—aunt, Florence Hamble."

"Any relative of Edith or Brock's is a friend of mine. It's nice to meet you, Mrs. Hamble."

"It's nice to meet you, too, Damon. I recognize your name. You're helping Brock with his Herrington campaign, correct?"

"Yes, I am. Edith and Greggory were a great help to me at the city fair on Wednesday."

"I'm so glad. It looks like the two of you have some catching up to do. If it's okay, Edith, I'll leave you here to help Damon and Brock for a few minutes while I pick up a surprise for you."

"Oh, I don't know if…"

"That's a great idea, Mrs. Hamble. Edith is exactly the kind of help I need today."

"Great, I'll be back in an hour. Have fun, Edith." Mother cuts through the crowd of people to give Brock a hug before she leaves.

I glare at my mother as she walks away from me. How did this happen? "Uh, what do you need help with, Damon?"

"Well, we're running low on buttons and pamphlets. If you could refill these tables with the things from the boxes below them, that would be a great start, and then if a hard-nose comes around, I might sic you on them. You know how to get anyone to vote for Brock."

"Okay," I say unenthusiastically as I pull out a box of pamphlets. Damon watches me as he hands a new stack of pamphlets to each of his volunteers. Once I have a big pile of 'Vote for Hamble' buttons on each of the three tables, I look longingly at my brother, Brock. He has at least 15 people standing in a line to talk to him. What a shame. I could use a brotherly hug right about now.

As I'm daydreaming, I hear Damon call my name. "Edith, would you be willing to tell Mr. Athill here what Brock Hamble's stance on The Complex Law is?"

I shake myself out of my stupor. "Sure, I'd love t—" As I lift my head I find myself staring into the unsmiling face of the complex chief. Images of his broad shoulders and skinny waist marching through my dorm each year, scowling at my friends and me fill my mind. I feel beads of sweat forming on my forehead. I force my gaping jaw shut as I meet his gaze.

"W-what would you like to know, Mr. Athill?"

The man's black hair that is usually stuck to his head appears to be unsticking on the left side. My eyes keep drifting to the horizontal tweaker as he speaks. "I am the most important employee at the Herrington Complex of Undesirables. I will not vote for anyone who might even possibly be against the system that I hold so dear."

Damon looks at me wearily as I feel one of the beads of sweat slide in front of my right ear. I clear my throat. "If you have read this pamphlet that outlines Brock Hamble's stance on all current laws, you will see that he is neutral on the Complex Law."

"Yes, I have read that, but I have reasons to doubt his— neutrality."

I feel the hairs on the back of my neck stand up. I can't mess this up. There is so much at stake. "Mr. Athill, I assure you that Brock Hamble wants to represent the people. The people voted for the Complex Law, so he upholds that law as the mayor of Adanlay, and he will continue to uphold that law as a senator for The United Cities."

The man lifts his nose in disdain. "I've heard rumors that there are people trying to bring down the Complex Law; will he support that kind of rebellion?"

A second bead of sweat slides down the other side of my face. "Brock Hamble is a representative of the people of the United Cities. If the majority of the people demand that the Complex Law be repealed, he will listen to them. I think you are worried about nothing though, sir. Look around you. Do you see any complex haters or rebellions? No. Of course not." I hand the complex chief a pamphlet and a button. "Reread the pamphlet and set your heart at ease. Please vote for Brock Hamble on Tuesday, and have a nice day."

The complex chief glares at me and throws the button on

the table with a *clank*. "I still don't believe he's neutral. His sister is on the loose from the complex. I will not be voting for him, and until his sister is captured—I will not have a nice day." He turns his back on me and storms away. I brace myself against the table as my strength gives out. That was terrifying.

I feel someone put their hand on my back. Damon's voice says, "Are you okay, Edith? You're shaking."

"I-I'm fine."

"I'm pretty sure that Mr. Athill is the Herrington Chief for the Complex of Undesirables. I've never met him in person until now. What a jerk."

"Yeah, he is."

Damon looks at me curiously. "Have you met him before?"

I wipe the sweat off my forehead with my fingertips. "Yes, I have met him before, unfortunately."

"That's surprising. You're from Trenton, aren't you?"

Oh shoot. "Yeah, I am. I, uh, met him at a party with my uncle once."

Someone turns me around and wraps their arms around me. It's Brock. He whispers in my ear, "I've been watching him linger around my line for the last half an hour. Are you okay?"

"I whisper back, "That was the scariest thing I've experienced since…"

My brother stops me from saying more. "He's gone now. You did well. I've got to get back." Damon's eyes narrow as he watches our hug.

"Thanks, Brock," I say as he lets go of me.

Damon claps Brock on the back as he leaves and says, "You've got this in the bag, my friend; you're at 60% of the popular vote and still going up."

Brock smiles. "Yeah, things are looking great. Thanks for all your hard work, Damon. I've got to get back to the line."

"No problem." Damon's attention turns back to me, and he hands me a bottle of water. "Sit down and take a drink. You look like you're going to pass out."

I sit down gladly. "I'm sorry. I'm having a rough day. I might not be the best of help for you right now."

He sits down next to me. "Your cousin was sure worried about you. What's wrong?"

How much can I say? He seems like someone I can trust, but I thought I could trust Jefrey too. "I—my best friend is very sick. I'm worried about her."

Damon puts his hand on my knee. "What kind of sickness? Hasn't she seen a doctor?"

I shift to the side so Damon's hand slips off my knee. "She's under the care of a doctor. She went through a traumatic experience and she's unconscious. I'm afraid she won't wake up."

"What kind of traumatic experience? A car wreck or something?"

I don't meet his eyes. "Yeah, something like that. I don't

really want to talk about it. I just want her to wake up and be okay."

Damon looks at me intently. "You are such a mysterious person. I find you so intriguing." Damon pats my knee briefly. "I hope your friend is okay."

"Thank you."

"Edith, are you ready to go?" my mother asks as she approaches us with multiple bags slung over her shoulders.

"Yes. I'm ready." I stand up and take some of the bags off my mom's arms.

Damon follows me around the table. "Can I carry those to your car for you?"

"Yes."

"No," I say at the same time, and more loudly than my mom.

Mother scrunches her eyebrows at me. "Uh."

I don't let her speak. "We've got it. Thank you anyway, Damon. Get more people to vote for Brock. See you later."

Damon looks disappointed. "Will I see you at our banquet the day of the vote?"

I look at my mom, who nods at me. "Yes. I'll be there. Have a nice day."

"You, too. I'm sorry about your friend, Edith."

"Yeah, thanks."

As we walk away, my mother waves at Brock then leans close to my ear. "You told him about Avra?"

"He could tell something was wrong. I didn't tell him any details. Just that I'm worried about my sick friend."

She turns around and takes one last look at Damon. "He's watching us walk away. I think he's interested in you."

I scowl. "That's what Greggory thinks too."

"What are you going to do about it?"

I am silent until we get loaded into the car. "I am an escapee from the complex, Mom. He can't get too close to me. I'm trying to discourage him."

"I bought you a new dress! It's purple. Do you want to see it?"

"No, not now."

Mother is silent for a minute before speaking. "My dream for you is that someday—you'll have friends who know your secret, and—don't care."

"Keep dreaming, Mom. You'll never guess who I talked to at Brock's booth…"

Chapter 11

GREGGORY AND SCOTT IMPRESS ME with how gently they carry Avra up the stairs. Garth is carrying her IV pole and catheter bag right behind them. My mom thinks that more light and stimulus might help wake her up, so we are taking her to my mom's piano room for a little concert on this Sunday afternoon. Greggory looks super sharp in a dress shirt and tie. He went to church with my parents today. My mother was positively giddy about it; I guess it's been a while since he's done that.

Scott slides onto the couch in the piano room and Greggory sets Avra right next to him. Her head wants to flop around, so Scott lays it gently on his shoulder. I sit on the other side of Avra with some lotion so I can massage her hands like I do every day now. My mom sits at the big piano while everyone else fills in the other chairs. There isn't a chair for Garth, so he sits in front of me and leans against my legs.

Mother starts to play. The song she plays is beautiful and sad at the same time; it tugs at my heartstrings. Garth reaches back and squeezes my hand when he hears me sniff. The next song is faster paced with lots of tinkling sounds, thank goodness.

"This song always reminds me of a river or a waterfall," my dad says with a contented sigh.

I nod at him, but I just have to take his word for it. I've never seen a river or a waterfall. I look at Avra and hope that she will get to see one with me someday. I pop the lotion bottle open and apply some lotion onto my friend's brown, lifeless hands. As I rub it into her palms I say, "Avra, as soon as you get better, we're going to go on a trip to see mountains and waterfalls together. If they're anything like this song, it will be peaceful and beautiful." I swear I feel Avra's hand twitch in mine. "Scott, did you see that?"

"See what?"

"She twitched! Avra's hand twitched just now!"

Scott takes Avra's hand from me. "I didn't see it; are you sure?"

I take her hand back. "Yes, I'm sure."

Greggory leans forward excitedly in his chair. "I saw it. She definitely twitched. She might come out of this!" He slips off his chair and kneels next to Avra. Garth scoots over to make room for him. Greggory starts massaging her hand with me.

Scott frowns and covers her other hand possessively with his own. My dad gets up and looks at Avra's IV pole. "This is good news. If we see more movement from her, I'll give her another shot of adrenaline. It might give her enough energy to come out of this."

Mother stops playing to hear what we're saying. I shake my head at her. "No, don't quit playing. She twitched. This is working." Mother smiles and resumes playing.

Greggory leans closer to me and whispers, "What happened to Avra's hair?"

"It's part of her internal deformities. She's always had this problem, but she's never lost this much hair at once. I think the trauma of going back to the complex and being interrogated did this."

Rage fills Greggory's eyes. "I swear, I'm going to punch the next person who takes someone I care about to the complex."

I whisper quietly enough that Scott can't hear me. "You care about Avra?"

His cheeks redden. "Of course I care about Avra."

Father walks to the door. "I think we need something refreshing to drink. I'm going to make you all my famous strawberry-peach smoothies. Greggory, will you lend me a hand?"

"Uh, sure." My brother follows my dad to the kitchen reluctantly.

Scott leans over to me. "I don't like the way he looks at Avra. Why can't he find a girl of his own kind?"

I frown at my friend's boyfriend. "What do you mean by that?"

"You know, he can have any girl in this world. I can't."

"We are all 'of the same kind' Scott. You never know, even if the law doesn't change, you could end up with the girl next door to your parents' house, and Greggory could end up with…"

"Don't you dare say it, Elira."

"Okay, okay. Sorry. I'll tell Greggory to back off."

Ring, ring, ring. My mom stops playing the piano and goes into my dad's office to answer the phone. We fall silent so we can hear what she's saying from the next room over. "Hello? Oh, hi, Adelia. No. I never watch the news on Sunday. I want it to be a day of peaceful music and family… Oh, really? Is it still on right now? I'll turn it on. Thank you. Goodbye."

Mother rushes back into the piano room and turns on a tiny little television that I hadn't noticed before on the bookshelf. A big picture of Brock looking official is highlighted next to a smaller picture of me as an escapee from the complex and a slightly blurry black and white picture of—Greggory in a parking lot show up on the screen.

My mother puts a hand over her mouth. "My friend called to let me know that all of my children are on the news."

The news anchor's voice is raised. "As a community, we have to wonder how this kind of information about a candidate for the Senate has been kept quiet until now. If you're just tuning in, it has been revealed today that one of the candidates for the Senate, Brock Hamble, is not the only member of his family worthy of recognition. One of the six escapees from the Herrington Complex of Undesirables is none other than Elira Hamble, Brock Hamble's sister. Though two of the escapees were apprehended, Elira Hamble is still at large. One has to wonder if Brock Hamble knows where she is and is hiding information about her on purpose in order to win the election."

Garth looks at my shocked face and holds my hand. "Are you okay?" We hear a loud sound coming from the kitchen. It must be the smoothie maker.

My eyes narrow at the television. "Why did this have to come out two days before the election?"

The news reporter continues, "If you thought things couldn't get worse for Hamble, Elira is not Brock Hamble's only sibling. His brother, Greggory Hamble, whom you can see here in this security camera photo in the parking lot of a night club, appears to be buying illegal drugs. This photo was taken only 10 days ago. So this poses the question to all citizens of The United Cities, do we trust the governing of our country to a man who is connected to drug addicts and wanted persons? What do you think—"

Mother shuts off the television and stands before us silently for a moment. Her voice cracks, "We were so close. I don't know what this will do for his chances now. I'm so sorry, everyone."

Father and Greggory come in with trays of pink drinks. They seem confused by our frowns. "Who wants a smoothie?"

Chapter 12

MY MOUTH IS FULL of cold fruity smoothie, but I can't taste anything. I set my empty glass on the side table in the piano room and lay my head on Avra's shoulder. I want to cry, but I know I should be strong. We tried so hard. Brock was so close. I feel responsible for his downfall. I feel my head twitch. No, it's not my head that twitched, it's Avra's shoulder! "Dad! Avra's shoulder just twitched."

Father looks sad, but he forces a smile. "That's great, honey. Keep track of how many times she twitches for me, okay?"

"Okay."

My mother wipes a tear off her cheek. "Who did this?"

Greggory raises his glass. "Well, I would bet money that it's Brock's opponent, Bloxhouse. He knew he was about to lose the election. He had to dig up dirt in order to win."

My mother sighs. "I kind of wonder about Peace Officer Blackwell. He knows about Elira and he has access to drug investigations."

I shake my head. "I bet it was Mr. Athill, the complex chief. He hates all of us."

Ding dong. Mother stands up and looks around frantically. "Someone is here. Get Avra to the bunker. If you don't have your disguise on, get in the bunker too." Garth jumps to his feet to help Scott carry Avra down the stairs. Rocky grabs the IV pole. They hurry, but still move slowly down the stairs. I don't feel comfortable leaving someone waiting at the door this long.

Ding dong. Mother's eyes are in a frenzy as she looks at me. "Your eye is covered, just go in the piano room with Greggory as Edith. I'm going to let them in now."

I feel fear seize me. I haven't played Edith at home before. I—I just need to play my part; I'm their niece, I have every right to be here. "Okay. Let them in."

Greggory puts his arm around me and leads me to the couch in the piano room. He turns the little television back on. They are still talking about Brock Hamble's disgraceful family. "Are you okay, Elira?" he whispers.

I hold my hands together so he won't see them shaking

and whisper back, "I feel like all of my hopes and dreams for people like me have been flushed down the toilet. They are making the two of us sound like hardened criminals. They don't even know us, but now the whole country will hate Brock and our entire family."

Greggory strokes his chin. "I know. I just hope I don't lose my job over this. I want to air the video of the complex whether Brock wins or not. People need to know what's going on in there. I'm sorry they are running your name through the mud. As for me, I'm kind of used to being the disgrace of the family."

I twist my ring around my finger nervously. "Do you think the peace officers are here to question us?"

Greggory shrugs. "If it's peace officers, they're probably here to see if I prefer a fine or solitary confinement."

Anger boils through my veins. "That black-and-white photo is blurry. They don't know if you were buying drugs or a candy bar."

"Shh!"

We can hear a man raising his voice in the hall. "Please let me see her. I know she is staying with you."

Greggory frowns at me. "That sounds like your admirer, Damon."

Damon himself walks into the piano room with Mom and Dad beside him. Mother clears her throat. "Edith, Damon came here to see you. Are you comfortable with that?"

I shrug. "Yeah, sure."

Damon looks at my parents and then at me. "Edith, I need to talk to you—privately."

Mom and Dad's faces are tense as mother motions for Greggory to join them. "We need to talk in the kitchen, Greggory. Edith, just holler if you need us."

I stand up and smile more confidently than I feel. "Okay."

Damon has a weird expression on his face once we're alone. "I assume you've been watching the news." He points to the little television on the bookshelf.

"Yes. I'm ready to turn it off." I turn off the television and join him on the couch.

"So, did you know Greggory was a drug addict?"

I frown at him. "He's not a drug addict. I happen to know that he wasn't buying drugs for himself in that picture. He was buying them—for a friend."

"What friend? You?"

Rage burns inside of me. "No!"

Damon softens his tone. "You know who he bought them for?"

"Yes, but I'm not telling you who it is. That person is not an addict either, and no one in this family will buy illegal drugs again. I promise."

Damon looks at me apologetically. "I'm sorry. I didn't come here to lecture you. I know the people in your family are good people. I'm just frustrated that Brock has dropped 12% in the popular vote today."

I feel a sob trying to escape my throat. I swallow it down. "Do you think all hope is lost?"

Damon slaps his hands on his knees. "No, 48% is still close to half. I have my work cut out for me in the next two days, but I won't give up. You shouldn't either, Elira."

I freeze mid nose wipe. Did he just say my real name? "You mean Edith."

He looks at me closely, focusing on my makeup-covered eye. He lifts his hand, touches the side of my face, and with a scraping motion uncovers some of my purple birthmark. I see flesh-colored makeup on his fingers as his hand retracts. Oh, no. Damon looks at his fingers and then at me again. "I mean Elira."

Fear, sadness, embarrassment, and maybe relief all battle to show themselves on my face. I should say something, but what? Should I deny it? I think it's too late for that. "If you turn me in, Brock will lose for sure, Damon."

"I won't turn you in."

"Do you want money to stay quiet?"

Damon looks hurt. "No. I just want you to know that I know who you are, and—I don't care."

I think relief just won the battle. I let out a long sigh. "Really? I thought everyone in this world wants people like me locked in the complex."

Damon takes my hand. "You are so smart, beautiful, and

determined to make a difference; I wish there were more people like you in my world. I'd be stupid to turn you in."

I feel myself blush. "Thank you." His hand doesn't let go of mine. "I think you should know that I have a boyfriend, Garrett..."

"You mean, Garth?"

I scoot back on the couch a few inches. "How did you figure all of this out?"

Damon lets go of my hand and taps his fingers on his knee. "Well, you look like your parents to me, and the way you and Greggory tease each other, and your determination to bring down the complex made me wonder. When I saw your reaction to the complex chief and Brock's reaction to you facing that jerk, I knew my suspicions had merit. I looked up all the information I could about you. You are definitely more than a distant cousin around here—Elira."

I look down at my hands. "I don't know what to say. You are the first person besides my family and friends to know my secret."

His knees press into mine. "We're friends, aren't we? You can trust me. I want to help you be free; I want that more than you can imagine." How did he get so close to me?

I scoot back even more. "Like I said earlier, I have a boyfriend."

Damon's deep blue eyes look down at his hands. "I know,

but can we at least be close friends? You are the most interesting person I know; I want to know everything about you."

I roll my eyes. "Really?"

"Yes."

I smile, surprised by how enthralled he is. "I would like to be your friend. Thank you for keeping my secrets."

"Speaking of your secrets, is the friend you were worried about the other day here?"

"Yes. I'll tell you about that later. I have a lot to process today."

"I'm sure you do. I'm going to talk to your parents about some campaign things, and then I better get to work. If I come up with a plan to win the dropping votes back, will you help me?"

"Yes."

"Thank you." Damon and I stand up. "Can I have a hug, as a friend, Elira?"

I hesitate for a second. I don't want to get his hopes up, but he did say he's okay with being friends. "Yes. Thank you for accepting me as I am. That means more than you know."

His arms feel surprisingly good around me. He lets go and says, "You are perfect just the way you are."

Chapter 13

HUH. THAT WAS THE WEIRDEST conversation I have ever had. I don't know what to think. Damon knows I'm from the complex and he still likes me, maybe too much. I walk down the stairs with so much on my mind.

Someone wraps me in their arms when I get to the bottom. "Hey, beautiful, are you okay? Who's upstairs?" Garth says as he kisses my cheek.

How much should I tell him? "Damon, from Brock's Herrington campaign."

"Is everything okay?"

I squirm in place. "Well, not really. Brock has dropped 12%

in the popular vote, but the most shocking news is, he—figured something out."

"Who figured something out? Brock?"

Greggory runs down the stairs with reckless abandon just then and almost knocks us to the ground. "Ha ha! Damon knows you're my sister! What do you think about that?"

Garth frowns. "He knows you are a complex escapee?"

I nod and take his hands, hoping that he'll recognize the significance of this moment. "Yeah, and he says he doesn't care. He thinks I'm a good person just the way I am. He promises he won't turn me in. He wants me to keep helping him with Brock's campaign."

Greggory snickers. "It's because he likes you. I could see this coming a mile away."

"What?" Garth asks as he glares at Greggory.

"Hey, don't kill the messenger," Greggory insists as he raises his hands in surrender.

Garth looks at me with pain in his eyes. "Is this true, Elira?"

"Well, I don't know for sure, but I told him that I have a boyfriend, and he said that he just wants to be my friend."

Garth's frown doesn't leave his face. "Hmm."

"He wants me to be free, and I think we should have as many friends in the political world as possible right now."

Garth looks at me and touches the spot where Damon scraped the makeup off my birthmark. "Just as long as he's the kind of friend who can keep his hands to himself."

"Elira! Garth! Come quick! Avra just squeezed Scott's hand. I'm going to tell Dr. Hamble," Rocky yells as he rushes past us up the stairs.

I take my jealous boyfriend's hand and run with him to the bunker. When I look at Avra on her bunk, I don't see any great change, except that her chest is noticeably rising and falling with each breath now.

Scott is all smiles. "She just squeezed my hand! I think she's going to make it."

I kneel down beside her and put my fingers on her wrist. Her pulse is noticeably stronger than it has been since we brought her back. I whisper to her, "Avra, wake up. You're home and safe. Scott and I need you." I feel her arm twitch. "Where is my dad?"

His deep voice answers from behind me. "I'm right here. How many times has she twitched?"

"Four. She's twitched four times this afternoon. Will you give her a shot of adrenaline?"

Father pulls a syringe out of a small box; he was expecting this, I think. "Adrenaline has a better chance of working now than any other time. Expose her thigh for me." I pull my friend's nightgown up her leg and watch my dad pierce the skin of her thigh with the needle. I force my eyes to watch as he pushes in the plunger. My stomach flips upside down. When he's done, he caps the syringe and feels for her pulse. I watch her still face expectantly, but nothing happens. Scott starts massaging her

101

feet gently. I take the wet towel my mom keeps in here to wipe her with from time to time, and wipe her face. Still nothing. Feeling defeated, I sit next to Garth on the couch and lay my head on his shoulder.

He tilts my chin up with his finger. "Don't give up; she'll wake up on her own time."

"I hope so." Garth doesn't let my chin go, he leads my face closer to his and places his lips on mine.

"Ahem, I don't think this is the time or place for that," I hear my father say. I haven't opened my eyes yet. If I get my way, I won't open them either.

"It's not the time or place for what?" I hear a weak, tired voice ask.

I open my eyes and turn to see Avra's eyes open and staring at me. "Avra!" I jump off the couch and hurl myself on my friend.

"Ow! Not so tight, Elira. You're going to break me."

"I don't care. My dad will fix you up if I do. I thought you were dead."

Avra blinks her tired eyes over and over again. "So did I. I can't remember very much."

My father puts a hand on her forehead. "Don't try to remember everything right now, just try to stay awake."

"Can I have a drink?"

My dad looks looks around the room. "Sure. Scott would you get her some water and a straw?"

"Absolutely." Scott is back in a wink.

My dad feels Avra's pulse on her wrist as he says, "Avra, do you want to sit up on the couch?"

"Yes. But I need some help; my arms feel heavy."

He and Scott lift Avra's skeletal form out of the bed and shimmy her to the couch. I move the IV pole behind them. Scott sits next to her like he did upstairs. My dad sits on the other side of her to keep checking her pulse. He is thrilled when she holds her own head up. "There, try a little drink."

Avra takes a tiny sip of water, then lays her head on Scott's shoulder. "That's enough for now. My head is heavy."

"I'm sorry, Avra. We had Maxine give you a powerful drug that made you appear dead so we could get you out of the complex. It worked a little too well on you. It may take some time to get you back to normal."

"That's okay. Did Maxine give some to Jefrey too? I saw him in the needle room. He said he was sorry. He said the last thing he meant to do was hurt Elira."

Chapter 14

DAMON CALLS MONDAY MORNING with a plan. He wants as many of us as possible to walk door to door starting on the poor side of each local city with buttons and pamphlets explaining how the truth about Brock's siblings prove how normal he is. We want people to know that Brock is really, just like them. I am for it. I will do whatever it takes to get Brock elected. I want people like Avra never to be tortured. I want Shasta and maybe even—Jefrey out. I want all of us to be free.

Garth and Rocky want to help for sure. Scott says he'll stay with Avra. She had a little bit of oatmeal and orange juice this morning before falling back asleep, so we're all feeling optimistic about her recovery. My parents, Ernestine, and Greggory are helping too. The problem is having enough drivers to go to all the nearby little cities we want to cover. My mother is highlighting maps of the cities we were asked to cover for everyone. She gnaws on a pen in frustration. "I wish we had one more driver. Then we could cover all five cities Damon asked us to take care of."

Father looks at Garth. "Florence, I think we could trust Garth to drive around Herrington. Greggory can take Tolsa, since he lives there, Ernestine can take Trenton, I can take Lancen, and you can take Rosett."

"Are you sure?"

Garth speaks up. "I can do it. I'll follow all of the speed limits and signs, and if Elira comes with me, she knows the roads around the railroad tracks really well."

My mother shakes her head and covers her eyes with her hands. "I don't think that's a good idea."

My father sighs. "Florence, the election is tomorrow. Elira and Garth want Brock to win. They won't fool around with the small amount of time we have left. Right?"

I look as seriously as I can at my parents. "Right."

Garth agrees with me. "Right."

Mother throws up her hands in surrender. "Fine. Who is Rocky going with?"

Ernestine pipes in. "Me. Of the five, Trenton is the next-biggest city to Herrington. I'll need his help. In fact, I may be able to get Frank to help, too."

Mother nods. "Okay, it's settled. Everyone make your disguises as different as possible today. We don't want anyone connecting you to this house if we can help it. Go upstairs and get sack lunches and dinners for yourselves from Freda. We'll meet back here at 9:00 pm. I can't express to you how important this is. We have today and then it's voting time. Let's give our all for 12 hours and then we'll let the chips fall where they may."

"Who's going to spill chips?" Rocky asks.

Mother frowns. "Never mind. I'll call Damon to confirm the cities he's assigned us. I hope he can find volunteers for every city."

GARTH AND I CLIMB INTO MY CAR. Today I'm thankful that my parents have so many cars. We watch as my mother leaves in her sports car. My dad leaves in his gray car, Ernestine leaves in the black car, and Greggory leaves in his blue sporty-looking car.

Garth leans over and gives me a kiss. "It's time to get to work. Do you know where you want to start?"

"Yes, by Avra's parent's house."

"Okay, let's go."

I help Garth get to the housing additions by the railroad

tracks without a problem. "Here is a stack of pamphlets. I'll take the right side of the road; you take the left."

"Okay, I guess we'll meet back here when we're done." He leans close to me for a quick kiss.

I wish our time together could be less busy, but we only have 12 hours to tip the balance so Brock wins. I will do what I can. I walk to the first house on my side of the street and knock on the door. I am curly red-headed Josie today. When the door opens, my smile and words are ready. "Hello, my name is Josie and I am here to remind you to vote tomorrow."

The balding, overweight man who answers the door looks at me curiously. "My vote doesn't matter. I don't have a job. I don't have my kid anymore. No one in the government wants me anywhere near a voting booth."

"That's exactly why you should vote. Brock Hamble knows how you feel. The government took his sister to the complex fourteen years ago. He's tired of seeing families ripped apart."

"I didn't say my kid went to the complex. How did you know?"

I smile at him. "It was a guess. What is your child's name?"

"Uh, James."

"Just between you and me, I know that Brock thinks the complex system is outdated and needs to end. He wants his sister Elira and your James to be free. The only way he can make that happen is if people like us get out tomorrow and vote for him."

He looks skeptical. "Are you sure he wants to change the law?"

I nod enthusiastically. "Yes, I am. He told me himself."

The man scratches his shiny head. "He wants to let my James out?"

"Yes, he does."

The man's eyes look a little bit teary. "Okay. If my car starts, I'll vote for him tomorrow."

The next house has a blonde woman with greasy hair and dull eyes behind the door. "Hello. I am here to ask you to get out and vote tomorrow."

"It's drug drop-off day tomorrow. My husband will be… It won't be safe for me to leave the house tomorrow."

I feel so bad for her. I reach out and squeeze her arm. "Have you seen what they're saying about Brock Hamble on the news lately?"

She smirks at me. "He isn't as squeaky clean as he seems."

"You're right, he isn't squeaky clean. He's human, just like you. What's your name?"

"Madge."

"Madge, Brock Hamble knows what it's like to have drugs affect his family. He wants to help people like his brother and your husband come clean from their addictions. He's just like us. If you get out and vote tomorrow, he will change things. He will change the laws that keep us prisoners in our own country. Would you like that, Madge?"

109

"Yeah, actually, I would."

"Find a good time to get out of here unnoticed, and vote for Brock." I feel sorry for stretching the truth, but I didn't say Greggory is a drug addict, just that he has an addiction of some kind.

The woman nods at me determinedly. "If I can get out of here unnoticed, I will vote for him."

"Thank you so much, Madge."

I pause when I get to the yellow house I have memories of dropping Avra off at. My knuckles are braver than my brain. *Knock, knock.* The man that I know to be Avra's dad opens the door a few inches. He looks at me cautiously and then looks at my car. I think he recognizes it. "I know who you are behind the red curls. I didn't do it."

"I know, Mr. Brown. May I please come in?"

He looks down both sides of the street before he lets me in. "Okay, but I can't do anything to help you."

I slip in the door before he can change his mind. "I know you didn't turn Avra in for the money. Our friend, or used-to-be-friend, Jefrey, did."

Avra's dad pulls a hard, wooden chair away from the battered table in the corner and squeezes the top of it with his hands. "The peace officers keep a close watch on me now. I wish I could help her, but I can't." He gestures for me to take a seat on the couch that has lost some of its stuffing since the last time I was here.

I sit down slowly on the broken couch. "I only have one thing I need help with, and that is your vote for my brother, Brock Hamble, for the senate tomorrow. He wants to repeal the Complex Law. He wants Avra and me to be free.

Mr. Brown covers his eyes with his hand. "She didn't look too good when they took her away. I don't know if she is still alive."

I lean forward. "She is. We broke her out, and she's alive. She's terribly weak, but she's alive."

Mr. Brown sits down on the hard kitchen chair. "She's alive. Will she be okay?"

"She'll get better sooner if we get the law changed. She'll be able to walk outside in the fresh air and come and go as she pleases."

Avra's dad narrows his eyes at me. "I haven't heard anything about a breakout."

"It's a long story, but they think she's dead and buried, but she's not."

Mr. Brown looks at me with his mournful eyes and chuckles. "You do beat all, little girl. I want to see her again."

I don't think that is a good idea. "I'm sorry, but she's too weak to walk right now, but when she's better I'll bring her to visit. Will you and your wife vote for Brock tomorrow?"

"If he will change the Complex Law, then yes. We will do it."

I stand up. "Thank you. That's all I can ask."

Avra's dad takes my hand and shakes it slowly. "Please take care of my Avra for me."

"I will."

An hour later I meet Garth back at the car. He smiles at me. "I think I convinced half of my side to vote for him."

"That's great," I say as I scratch beneath my wig.

He takes my hand and kisses it. "How did it go for you?"

"I convinced all but one."

Garth sets my hand down slowly. "Wow. Good job. You have more flair for this than I do."

I allow myself a little bit of pride when I say, "I'm just getting started. Ten hours to go! I'm having a soda. Would you like one?"

Chapter 15

"I'M SORRY, MA'AM, what you're saying sounds great and all, but I am Leonard Bloxhouse's great-uncle once removed. I have to vote for him or I'll get kicked out of my family."

"I understand, sir. You have to vote for Bloxhouse, even if he wants to keep everything we all hate about the government the same. You have a nice day now." The elderly man looks bewildered as I smile and wave goodbye to him.

Garth overhears that last conversation as he joins me on the sidewalk. "Man, you lay the guilt on thick, don't you?"

I snicker as I plop into the passenger seat of the car,

completely exhausted. "It was my last house. I wanted to end on a win."

Garth yawns as he pulls out onto the road. "So, what do you think? Is Brock going to win tomorrow?"

I shove a stale cookie in my mouth right as he asks his question; I answer him with my mouth full. "I don't know. I convinced a lot of people who were disgusted with his siblings to still vote for him, but I don't know if it's enough."

Garth takes my hand. "I would say the houses I visited were about 50/50 for and against him. It's going to be close."

I open my map and look at the nearest road sign. "Do you know where to turn? It's hard to see in the dark."

"Yeah, I'm just going back the way we came."

"You remember all of that?"

"Of course, don't you?"

"Um, mostly, but I've been to Avra's parents' house a few times. This is your first time on this side of town, isn't it?"

"Yep."

My heart fills with pride for my boyfriend. "Your memory is amazing."

Garth smiles and shakes his head. "Your ability to get people to see things your way is amazing."

I think about my dad's hands and Avra and frown. "Whatever."

Garth squeezes my hand. "What's the matter?"

"When we escaped from the complex, I felt like a leader

even though I didn't want to be. I made myself be strong for Avra's sake. Now I want to be a leader. I want to make this world fair for everyone, but I am a terrible driver, I'm responsible for both Avra and my dad's injuries, and I couldn't even stand up to the complex chief while in disguise the other day. I can't even find my way back home. I'm not a leader after all."

Garth comes to a stop at a stop sign and turns to me. "Wait a minute. I remember what you said you told the complex chief; that took guts. You got the peace officer off everyone's trail the day we took Avra back. You just convinced almost every house you visited, for 12 hours straight, to vote for your brother. You have Jefrey, me, and probably Damon, from the sound of it, following you around like puppy dogs. That sounds like someone being a leader to me."

"When I think of a leader I think of someone like Brock, who is loved and admired by the people."

"That's funny, because I just see him as a smiling face that represents the true unseen leaders who stand behind him."

I shake my head in bewilderment. "Who are the leaders who stand behind him?"

"Your parents and Ernestine, for starters."

I wave my hand dismissively. "You just have a parent-worship thing going on. They aren't leaders."

Garth is silent for a moment. "Did I include my parents in that list? No, I didn't. Don't get me wrong, they are good people, but they don't stand up for what they believe in—like your parents do."

I throw my hands up in exasperation. "No one but us knows what they do; I don't know if that is leading."

"Some leaders, like your mom, don't need to be seen to do the right thing and convince others to do the same."

"But is what she's doing changing the world?"

"It's changed my world, and yours, and Avra's, and Freda's."

I pause as I think about that. "I guess you're right. My dad seems so quiet to me, but he came up with the plan to save Avra's life. That was being a leader, right?"

"Yes! Think about Ernestine. She helped us escape and found my parents even at great cost to herself. She's been trying to start this rebellion for years. She's a leader, too."

I find myself deep in thought. "I never realized how many different kinds of leaders there are."

"It takes all kinds of leaders to connect with people and make things happen. Even Greggory is showing some leadership these days. He's going to get the country on our side."

We pull up to my parents' house with so much on our minds. I imagine my brother, who was a selfish jerk just a few months ago. "Yeah, he said he would put the tape on even if it cost him his job and even if Brock doesn't win." I gather up the few remaining pamphlets in the car and stuff them in a bag. "I sure hope Brock wins tomorrow."

Chapter 16

EVERYONE BUT AVRA AND SCOTT are going to Brock's banquet at the Herrington Event Center to watch how the vote turns out. I am going as Josie again. My nerves are extremely on edge. The consensus of our group is that our door knocking turned out about 50/50. It could go either way.

I give Avra a hug before I leave. She is on the couch in the great room for the first time since we broke her out. She takes my hand in her skinny one. "I wish I could go with you, Elira, but I don't think I'll be able to walk for a few days yet."

"I wish you could come too, but it'll be more comfortable

for you here. We'll have to be careful not to get on camera too much. That would give us all away."

Avra whispers into my ear, "Greggory says that someone named Damon will be there, and he likes you."

I roll my eyes. "Yes, he will be there, but he said he was fine with being friends."

"Is Garth fine with you two being friends?"

I bite my lip. "Not incredibly. Wish me luck. This is going to be a long, awkward night."

The old Avra is coming back, I think. She smiles at me. "Good luck."

Ernestine, disguised as a man, takes Rocky with her in the black sedan. Greggory decides to ride with the rest of us in my car. He makes sure I feel like an Elira sandwich when he shoves his way into the back with Garth and me. "Get off me, Greggory!"

"Oh, sorry."

When we get to the Herrington Event Center, Douglas Shriner meets us at the door. "Barry, let these fine people in. This is Brock Hamble's parents and brother, and Doctor Hamble's assistant, Josie, and I believe, her boyfriend, Mick."

"I'll still have to check their bags, sir."

"If anyone isn't here to cause trouble, it's the candidate's family," Shriner mumbles as the peace officers check our bags.

My dad smiles. "It's okay. Safety first. I'm impressed that you remembered our names; what a fine memory you have."

Mr. Shriner smiles proudly. "Thank you, I try. Is your niece Edith coming tonight?"

"Uh, I don't think so, she said she was feeling under the weather tonight and wasn't sure she should be out and about."

"That's too bad. I know my vice president, Damon, was looking forward to seeing her tonight, if you know what I mean." Douglas elbows my dad in a friendly way.

Dad laughs as he eyes Garth. "Oh well, another time."

Garth frowns as he escorts me into the event center. "Which one is he?"

My mouth goes dry. "Garth, I told him you're my boyfriend. He said he just wants to be my friend."

"I know. I trust you, but I don't trust him."

"Be nice to him. He's a good person, and we need his help if we're going to change the law."

"Introduce me to him."

I sigh. "Okay." I take Garth to the stage where Damon's back is to us as he sets up a microphone. I clear my throat loudly to get his attention. "Hello, Damon. I don't know if you remember me, but I am Josie, Edith's friend."

Damon narrows his eyes at me and then smiles. "Of course I remember you. Is this Garrett?"

I smile. "Close, this is Garrett's friend, and my boyfriend, Mick."

Damon offers his hand to Garth. "It's a pleasure to meet you."

Garth pauses for a split second and then takes Damon's hand. "I'm pleased to meet you too, finally." Their handshake should be breaking apart now, but it isn't.

I clear my throat. "We were able to visit over half of Herrington yesterday, Damon. Which city did you knock doors at?"

Damon lets go of Garth's hand but keeps his eyes locked on him. "I covered most of Watercrest yesterday. I finished at almost 10 last night. I'm tired. I hope I last all night."

Garth looks around the room. "This party is going all night?"

"Well, at least midnight or one, I'd say."

"I hope there's enough food to keep us awake."

"There is. It cost twice as much as we had budgeted because Brock said he didn't want to use Complex Catering anymore. He covered the extra cost himself."

I smile, grateful that my brother is taking a stand against unfairness to people like me. "It looks and smells delicious. Is now the best time to eat?"

"Yes. It's 7:00 now, and the votes will start rolling in around 9:30; we should know the final count by 11:30 or midnight. So, eat up. I'll join you if I get a minute."

I say as sincerely as I can, "Thanks for inviting us and for your quick thinking yesterday."

Damon shrugs. "I just hope it was enough."

Garth and I fill our plates with chicken, potatoes, and salad and sit down next to Rocky and Ernestine. "Do you think the peace officers at the door recognized us?" I ask in a whisper.

Ernestine swallows before answering me. "No. They are too busy checking purses and briefcases to focus on faces." We change the subject when a group of business men and women fill in the rest of the seats at our table.

A large woman with a gray bun smiles at all of us. "There are a lot of people here. Every seat is full; it's going to be standing room only for the people still getting checked at the door."

A man with a thick black mustache says, "That is a good sign for Hamble, I think."

A woman with a huge blonde mane of hair and red lips says, "Time will tell."

Ernestine finishes her food and leaves to talk to 'the mother of the candidate.' Damon takes her seat. "So, is everyone ready to see Brock win?"

"Is the man himself going to make an appearance here tonight?" the man with a thick black mustache asks.

Damon wipes his mouth with his napkin and nods. "Yes. He is spending the first half of the night in Adanlay and the second half here."

I look at Damon curiously. "Isn't it a five-hour drive from Adanlay?"

"Yes, but he is taking the high-speed monorail. It's less than an hour commute that way."

The large woman with a gray bun says, "I didn't think it was open for business until next week."

"It's not open to the public yet, but government officials started using it a few days ago."

The woman with the gray bun frowns. "Hmm, what other niceties do government officials get that we don't?"

Damon swallows quickly. "Oh, not many, I'm sure. The biggest perk is that they can leave the country and get to decide who else can do the same."

A thin man with a bushy black beard says, "I've heard a rumor that former Presidents of the United Cities haven't gone into the Complexes for the Elderly when they've turned 80, and that Alexander Prystine won't go to the complex on his birthday either."

Damon shakes his head. "Rumors are rarely true, Mr. Neilson."

Mr. Neilson leans forward conspiratorially. "My cousin's housekeeper cleans for many upscale homes in Adanlay. She told my cousin that she's seen with her own eyes our former President, Thomas Kindercade, in a wheelchair in his son's basement when she was cleaning there."

The man with the black mustache says, "If that's true, then that may mean presidential families are keeping their flawed children out of the Complex of Undesireables too."

"Oh, I've heard from this same cousin that her housekeeper

saw an eighteen-year-old boy with an unusually small, stocky body in the same basement."

The woman with the gray bun pushes herself back from the table. "If the President feels himself above the Complex Law, what else does he feel himself above?"

Damon shrugs. "The boy may have been in an accident. It is possible."

Mr. Nielson folds his arms across his chest. "I don't think so."

I butt in. "That's why we're all here tonight, isn't it? Brock Hamble can see the injustice of the Complex Law and the existing government officials; he wants to change things so the laws are fair to everyone."

Damon looks at me sideways. "I don't know that he has written anything official about this."

I shrug even though Damon and Garth are glaring at me. "Voting is over. Whether he wins or loses, there's no reason to deny the facts. He wants the law to be fair to all."

Mr. Shriner taps the microphone to get our attention. "Hello, everyone. We're glad you all came to celebrate the election of the best future-senator this country has ever seen!" Thunderous applause erupts throughout the room. "Brock Hamble himself will join us in about an hour. The city voting totals should start coming in shortly after that. We will keep a tally of the votes for both Hamble and Bloxhouse on the screen to my left as they come in. In the mean time, how would you like to hear from our candidate's father?" The answering applause is deafening.

My dad takes the microphone from Mr. Shriner and waves at the crowd. I notice that he still has a bandage on each hand. "It's an honor to be here tonight with all of you to celebrate my son, Brock Hamble, the soon-to-be senator for the United Cities!" I worry that our hands are going to wear out with all of this clapping.

I lean over to Damon. "Did Dr. Hamble know he was going to give a speech?"

Damon nods at me. "He was asked to relieve everyone's minds about Elira and Greggory."

My eyes bulge. "Are you sure he's up to a task like that?"

Damon nods to my father. "Ready or not."

My father smiles at the crowd in his kind, soft-spoken way. "I know you have all seen the news the past two days. My son Greggory was shown on a camera appearing to buy illegal drugs. I want you all to know that he has fought with addictions of various kinds in the past, but he is clean and doing well. We are a real family and we are far from perfect. I hope we aren't the only people in this room who can say that." People around me laugh out loud. Father goes on. "He wasn't buying for himself in that photograph, and whether that was a good idea or not, I stand by him and assure you that he has my trust and confidence." The applause isn't as loud as before, but people are still liking what they are hearing in general.

"As for our daughter, Elira…" The room falls unnaturally quiet. "We—were heartbroken when she was taken away from us over 14 years ago. She was taken because she had a purple birthmark over one eye. That flaw she had—was only skin deep." The woman with the gray bun at my table wipes her eye. I hear sniffling behind me. "The news has let it be known that she has escaped The Complex of Undesirables and is living as a fugitive." Father glances at me only briefly. "I am a law-abiding, helpful citizen of my community and this country. However, what I say next, I say simply as a father. Wherever she is—I hope she is all right. I don't have anything more to say about that." I take a quick look around me. People are moved by his words. I'm so—relieved that people aren't cursing my name. Father switches gears. "Brock knows what it's like to grow up in a family with flaws. Some in this country believe that all flaws have been removed from our society, but that is not true. All of us have a flaw of one kind or another—either physical, mental, or emotional. Brock has learned from the flaws in our family and has become a man whom I am proud to claim as my son. He is my first-born son, he is a leader, and an all-around good person. Our country will see justice and moral reasoning brought back to the government when he is elected. Thank you all for supporting my son, and God bless you." People all around me jump to their feet and clap louder than ever.

Garth leans over and whispers in my ear, "I told you he was a leader."

I struggle to contain my emotions. I have to be Josie even though my pride is spilling over. He is a leader; the kind people will follow.

Mr. Shriner approaches the microphone. "Thank you, Doctor Ross Hamble, for your inspiring words. And now, ladies and gentlemen, I present to you the man of the hour, Brock Hamble!" My hands are definitely getting sore from all of this clapping. Brock looks good. The stress he's feeling is showing a little bit, but his smile is bright, and he looks like he is ready to conquer the world.

"Hello, Herrington, the city of my youth! I hope you've met my parents and brother here tonight. They have supported me and taught me how to be the man I am today. The high-speed monorail between Adanlay and Herrington is in fine working order. Your tax dollars have gone to good use. Make sure to try it out when it opens to the public next week. It made it possible for my family and me to be in both the presidential city and my hometown this evening. I'd like to introduce you to my wife, Chantilly, and my daughter, Joy."

Chantilly smiles and waves at everyone. Joy hides behind her pregnant mother's leg. Brock leads his wife to the microphone. She takes the front and center of the stage like it's nothing at all. "Hello, Herrington! What a warm and wonderful welcome we've had here. My husband is excited to celebrate his election in his hometown! Thank you all for voting for him and promoting his campaign. We couldn't have come this far without you." Chantilly sees Mr. Shriner inching toward her on the stage, so she backs away and waves as she goes.

Mr. Shriner waits for the applause to die down before addressing the audience. "If I can have everyone's attention, the smallest city in the country, Drotmire has tallied their votes and they will appear on the screen any minute now. Ah, here they are." My eyes are drawn to the screen. Oh no. "52% of the vote goes to Bloxhouse and 48% goes to Hamble.

Damon watches my face sink. "Don't worry, there are only 5,000 votes in Drotmire. The balance will flip and flop with each city reporting."

Before I can reply, the statistics change. Mr. Shriner smiles and points to the screen, "And another city, it looks like Watercrest, has reported their votes. Things are looking pretty even so far." Bloxhouse has 51% and Hamble has 49% now.

I lean toward Damon and say, "So, tell me, did we have volunteers knocking doors in every city yesterday?"

"I sent people to every city but Adanlay."

I understand that. "Good. Brock's own city is a for-sure thing. They like him as mayor."

THE TALLY BOARD BLASTS its bright red and blue colors into my brain. Hamble 40%, Bloxhouse, 60%. I try not to despair, but I really thought it would be closer this late into the night. There are only two cities left to report and they are both big ones, Herrington and Adanlay. They are both 'home cities' to Brock, but will it be enough to overcome a 10% deficit?

"Everyone, if I can have your attention please, Herrington city hall has just called us with the result of their votes. They should appear on the screen any moment now."

I feel like my head is pulsing louder than my heart. Just put it up; I need to know. I look down at my hands right as the results appear. The cheering brings my head back up, Bloxhouse, 56%, Hamble 44%. Oh. That's good. It's the right direction, but that's not enough to win. I lay my head down on the table gently, so I don't disrupt my wig. My eyes close. We worked so hard and I was so sure that Brock would win a week ago. I don't think he can jump 7% with only Adanlay left. His hometown only brought him up 4%.

Garth whispers to me, "Let's get out of here for a minute."

"Okay." I try to look as dignified as Josie should under the circumstances as we walk past the peace officers and drink in the cold night air. We walk far enough away that they can't overhear us, yet we can hear Mr. Shriner trying to console the audience over the microphone.

Garth hugs me in the cold night air. "Are you okay?"

I sob, "No. I don't think we can do it without him."

Garth wipes a tear off my cheek. "Greggory is still going to do his part."

"I know, but I don't think it will be enough by itself."

Damon walks out the door toward us at a brisk pace. "The call from Adanlay just came in. Get in here."

I wave him away. "I can hear the microphone just fine out here."

Damon reaches his arm out toward me. "We started this thing strong; let's finish it strong."

I shrug. "Okay, fine."

Garth keeps himself between Damon and me as we walk back in.

Mr. Shriner tells us what we already know. "This is it, ladies and gentlemen. Please direct your eyes to the screen."

The whole room goes silent. Damon sits down at our table and sets his head on his arms. He already knows. He must be so disappointed. I sit down next to him to console him when the room erupts into applause. What? I look at the screen and see the number 51% next to—Hamble! 49% Bloxhouse. No way. How did Adanlay pull him up 7%?

I laugh in triumph even though I'm so confused. "I thought you said you didn't send anyone to Adanlay."

Damon raises his head off the table. "I didn't. Brock and Chantilly went door to door themselves."

I jump out of my seat and hug Garth. "We did it! It's a miracle, but somehow we did it!"

My mom and dad rush over and wrap their arms around me. Greggory is laughing like a maniac when he joins us. I'm even more impressed when Brock breaks away from the throngs of people around him and completes our family hug. Their tears trigger mine. Brock voices what we're all thinking. "I can't believe it! We won!"

Chapter 17

AVRA SMILES AT ME from her side of our bed. "I wish I could have been there."

"I know. I wish you could have, too. How are you feeling?"

Avra smirks. "Like the walking dead."

I laugh and then grow somber. "So tell me about being back there."

She sighs and lays back on the pillows. "It was horrible. The complex chief, Mentor Briggs, Mentor Roberta, and Doctor James came to my cell to yell at me every day. I just sat there and didn't say anything. The food was way worse than the pink trays I remember. It tasted so weird and I quit caring about everything. I was so sad to be away from everyone I love and back to the place that I knew would kill me that I just let myself shut down."

"I'm surprised they thought they could get answers from you while medicated on their new concoction of behavior modification stuff."

"They realized after a while that the medicine was keeping them from their goal. They took me off all medicine for a few days and then stuck me in a room with Jefrey. I think they were hoping that if the two of us were together that we would talk about where the rest of you were."

I could see how that would work. Fear seizes me. "Did you two talk then? Did you give anything away?"

"Jefrey knew what they were doing. He told me not to say anything about this place. He said they planned to kill us both no matter what, so it wasn't worth hurting the rest of you too."

Is this the same Jefrey who was angry and resentful when he left? "I'm so surprised to hear that. I mean, he sold us out not that long ago."

Avra stretches out on the bed. "I think he has changed, Elira. He apologized for turning me in for money. He said that he was mad that Garth was getting everything he wanted and he wasn't. Jefrey thought that if he had enough money then he could have everything he wanted, too. But that plan backfired on him. He lost everything, and he knew that you would never forgive him. That made him the saddest. He said that he never wanted to hurt you."

Wow. I'm thrilled to know that even villainous people have goodness in them. "It has been a heart-wrenching time, Avra. Knowing that my best friend was back in the place that would kill her and being betrayed by someone I used to care about left me—a mess."

Avra pats my hand. "Well, the good news is, Brock won today! Things are going to change for all of us. Are you ready to lead us into a newer new world?"

A laugh escapes my lips. "I won't be the one leading us anywhere. If everyone does their part, then no one person will have to lead us. Well, Brock will still have to be the smiling face of our little rebellion."

Knock. Knock. Who could that be? It's 1:30 in the morning. I wrap my robe tightly around myself and walk to the door. "Elira, I need to talk to you," Greggory says through the crack in the door.

"Okay, just a minute." I tuck Avra in and kiss her forehead before I leave. "Greggory wants a word with me. I'll be back soon."

"Okay, I'll try to stay awake," she says with a yawn.

I giggle as I watch her eyes blinking. "Good luck with that."

Greggory leads me to the couch in the great room. A single lamp dispels the darkness in the room. Everyone else is asleep. "So, Brock won."

I smile excitedly. "Yes. Our plan is going to work."

Greggory looks down at his hands. "I don't know about that."

What is he thinking? "Why? The video is ready. You just need to put it on the air in a couple of days."

"I wish I could, Elira."

No, he can't get cold feet now. "Why can't you?"

"I was just fired."

"What?"

"When we got back here, dad listened to a message on the answering machine. It was my boss firing me for my supposed drug addiction. He said he left a message at my apartment two days ago, but since I hadn't answered, and the news has proclaimed my family ties loud and clear, he called here."

This is not happening. We have to counteract it somehow. "Can you talk to him? I could talk to him. I pleaded your case all day Monday to people. I can do it again."

Greggory shakes his head. "No, it's too late. I don't want to make him any angrier than he already is."

"Does Mom know?"

"Yeah."

"What did she say?"

He grins as he recalls our angry mother's words. "She said I still have to do it when I go to clean out my desk."

"When are you going to do that?"

"Tomorrow."

My brain tries to make what we have to work with still work. "But Brock gets sworn in tomorrow; it's too soon. What happens if you wait a day?"

Greggory scoffs. "They'll throw away my stuff and refuse to let me enter the building."

Well, we have no choice then. "Yes. We can make it work. When do people watch the national news station the most?"

"What day?"

I roll my eyes. "No, what time of day?"

"Prime time is 7:00 pm."

"Good. Brock will be sworn in by then. Can you get the video on that late?"

Greggory rubs his messy blonde hair anxiously. "I don't know, maybe. I was told to get my stuff out by midnight tomorrow or lose it. So, they should let me in."

"You have to figure out how to get in that room and put the tape on. It's a day or two early, but if it's our only chance to get near the machines, we will make it work."

Greggory's eyes are agitated. "I want to do this, but I'll be making so many people there mad. What if I chicken out? Will you go with me?"

I won't allow Greggory to chicken out. Somebody should go with him. "I would love to, but I doubt Mom and Dad will let me."

My brother taps his fingers together. "We'll have to fib

a little to the parents, but I'm sure my boss will let my cousin Edith help me carry my stuff out."

I guess this means I'm going then. "What will happen when they see what we've done?"

His eyes narrow as he calculates how to do this. "I'll have to lock them out of the control room and once the video is done, we'll have to escape, probably through a window."

Oh boy, this is going to be intense. "If we don't get your stuff out with us, will you be okay without it?"

"Yeah, I don't have anything special there except a mug I really like."

"I'll get you a new one."

"You better."

Chapter 18

"BROCK HAMBLE, DO YOU SWEAR to represent the people of The United Cities in the second-highest of government offices and obey and uphold the laws of our country for the next 10 years?"

"Yes, I do."

Our pudgy little President, Alexander Prystine raises his deep voice so all can hear. "I now present to the people of the United Cities our newest senator, Brock Hamble!" He's acting pleased to have Brock now, but that is going to change tonight. I wish I could see his face when he finds out. The crowd around me erupts into applause. I feel like my own clapping does nothing to add to the roar, but I guess the roar wouldn't happen without each of us adding to it.

My parents are on the steps of the Adanlay National Government Office Building with Brock, Chantilly, and Joy. What a bunch of happy, beautiful people. I'm proud to be related to them, I've decided. This is a good day; I wish I could stay longer and savor this hard-earned victory, but I don't have time. There is a luncheon going on here in about a half an hour. I am not staying for it, though. Ernestine is taking Rocky, Garth, Brock, and me back to Herrington right now. We don't want to risk being seen and causing problems. We will be causing problems today, but this is not the time nor the place.

"MOM, GARTH AND I need to drop off a can of paint to Rocky's dad. We told him we would do that after the election."

I've never seen my mother so exhausted. She is sitting on the comfiest chair in the piano room with her feet up and a silky mask over her eyes. "It can wait until Ernestine can take you."

I was afraid of this. "No, I want to practice driving around the block a little bit, too."

Mother pulls her mask off. "Only if an adult goes with

you, and frankly, we're all exhausted from last night and this morning. You should be curling up on the couch with Avra to watch our video go live in an hour."

"Mom, I don't want to miss the video. I'll be quick. I just need to feel like I can do simple things on my own. Please? Let me have this one thing?"

My mother must be more tired than I think because she nods at me. "You have half an hour. Don't go anywhere risky. We need you ready for the next phase of our plan."

I can't keep my conniving smile on the inside. "Okay. Thanks, Mom." She pulls her mask back over her eyes.

I sneak into my dad's empty office and call a number I have on a little slip of paper. "Molly? Hello. This is Edith Westergard. We met at Brock Hamble's booth at the Herrington City Fair. Yes, it's good to hear your voice too. Anyway, something big is happening tonight. Watch the national news station at 7:00. We won't be the only ones disgusted with the Complex Law after tonight. We'll need your help. Are you willing? Great. Thanks. Bye." Here goes nothing.

Garth wraps his arm around me as we walk to the garage. "I can't believe she let us leave together."

"I think I'm finally more than a kid in her eyes—or maybe she was too tired to think straight." I sigh as we enter the garage. "That video is intense. People are going to freak out."

Garth hefts a can of white paint into the back of my purple car. "Are we really going to drop this off?"

"Yes. Frank needs all the supplies he can get for that house. You are going to drop me off at the national news station after that."

"Elira, why can't I stay with you?"

His pleading eyes are hard to resist. "It'll be too hard to explain why Greggory brought two people with him to clean out his desk. And it'll be too hard to get away."

Garth's eyes fill with concern. "Exactly. You shouldn't go. He can do it himself."

I don't want to tell Garth that my brother might lose his nerve on his own. "He says he needs another pair of hands."

Garth is not convinced. "I can be his other pair of hands."

"No, I want to do this. Please let me. I escaped the complex. I can escape an office building."

My boyfriend huffs out his exasperation. "Do they have peace officers there?"

I avoid his eyes. "No, but they will be called for once the video starts."

Garth shakes his head and cups the side of my face with his hand. "I don't know if I can leave you there."

I smile at him. "You can. I will be fine."

"If I don't have you back in my arms in a few hours, I will do something drastic."

"Deal."

I drive the short distance to Frank Moore's house. Garth takes the can of white paint inside to Rocky's dad. I am tempted to leave Garth here, so he won't do something stupid, but he'd probably walk home and tell my parents what I'm doing. I better just take him with me. As I pull back onto the road, I realize that this is the only drive I've tried on real roads. Garth squeezes my hand. "Do you know how to get to the national news station?"

I nod assuredly. "Yep. I remember from our date night."

My boyfriend lovingly takes my hand. "We need another one of those."

I sigh. "Yes, that sounds great, but work before play."

I decide to take the easiest route, which unfortunately, will take us past the complex. I keep my eyes on the road as I see the concrete monstrosity looming in front of me. I wonder what Shasta is doing behind those thick walls right now. Her blistered fingers might be showing bone, for all I know. Garth stares at the complex as he asks, "Do you think Jefrey is sorry for what he did?"

I have been thinking about the same thing since Avra woke up and told me he regretted hurting me. Our conversation last night convinced me that he has changed. "I bet he's sorry. His plan didn't turn out too well for him."

Garth haltingly asks, "Do you want to save him, Elira?"

I look at him and see the turmoil behind his eyes. "I—I want to save everybody. The real question is if he will let me—or us, I guess."

He looks at his hands. "Do you think he's worth the effort?"

Words start coming from my mouth that feel right somehow. "Everyone, even jerks and back-stabbers, deserves to be free." When did I decide that? "I can't think about him right now. I have a job to do in fifteen minutes."

Garth squeezes my hand. "What do I do after I drop you off?"

"Go home. I'll get a ride home with Greggory."

"Is he already there?"

I feel my nerves taking over. I barely miss a pole as I turn into the national news station. "He should be waiting in the parking lot." Oops. I better keep both hands on the wheel.

Once we're parked, my boyfriend peers out the window. "There he is." Garth takes my hand and kisses it. "Elira—I don't think I should leave you here."

"I'll be back in your arms in a few hours. I love you." I wrap my arms around him and press my lips to his. I try to let go, but he doesn't let me, so I stay in his arms. A knock on my window forces me away from the beautiful eyes and lips that always make me feel safe and wanted.

I hear in a muffled voice through the closed window. "Come on, sister. It's desk cleaning time." Greggory taps a small video tape against the window to reinforce his point.

I open the door and start to climb out until something stops me. Garth hurls himself into the driver's seat as he holds onto the edge of my jacket. "Whatever happens, get out. Don't let them take you back there." He looks worried.

"Okay, I will. I'll even break my toes if I have to." Garth laughs and pulls me in for one more kiss. I feel myself trembling as I climb out of the car after that. Garth waves as he drives away. He drives like he's been doing it for years. I hope I really do get to collapse in his arms in a couple of hours.

Greggory clears his throat. "No more gloomy face. You are my cousin now, and you're not sad; if anything, you are mad that I've been fired. Can you sell that to these people?"

I mentally switch gears. "Yeah, no problem. Let's go."

Greggory hands me an empty box that looks like the one he's carrying except there are two large packages of cinnamon rolls in his. I don't know what their significance is, but I enjoy the spicy scent of them as the two of us enter the national news station. A grouchy-looking, middle-aged woman looks up from her desk. "What are you doing here, Hamble? I heard you were fired for your illegal drug use."

"It wasn't for me, but Mr. Fronze doesn't believe me, so yeah, I'm fired. I just came to clean out my desk."

"Who's this? Your druggie girlfriend?" I can't help scowling at her.

Greggory pats my back. "No, of course not. This is my cousin, Edith. You should speak to us in a kinder way if you want a cinnamon roll."

The woman licks her lips as Greggory sets the fresh cinnamon rolls on the long, narrow desk top. "Well, let me know if you need help, Greggory, and—I'll call an intern for you."

"My cousin, Edith is here to help me. I'll be fine. Make sure everyone gets a cinnamon roll and knows that I will miss working here. Have a nice day, Winifred."

"Heh."

Greggory takes me around the corner to a big room full of office spaces that he calls cubicles. Heads start popping out of them and sniffing. At least three people leave their desks to follow the heavenly scent. Good thinking, Greggory. When we find his desk, I'm surprised to see a picture of my parents with Brock and Greggory on his desk. This can't be more than a year old. I pick it up and smile before I place it in the box I've been toting around. Greggory hands me another photo frame. Is this our family? It looks like my mom and dad when they were much younger. Brock is about twelve, Greggory is maybe six, and I—I am in this picture. My head is turned so you can't see my left side at all. I am a toddler, close to two. I look like a normal kid, with no deformities from this point of view. We are in a sunny, sandy place with funny looking trees. I wish I could remember this day.

I turn to my brother. "Can I have this?"

"No."

"Why not?"

"I like that picture."

"So do I. I've never seen it before."

"If you do something for me, I'll give it to you."

I roll my eyes. "What?"

My brother shrugs. "I'll tell you later. Put all these bottles in your box."

I frown as I start stacking long, skinny glass bottles in my box. "Dad said you quit drinking."

"I have."

"Then what are all these for?"

"My friends give them to me, and I've been stashing them in that drawer, so they aren't at home with me when the temptation strikes."

"That actually makes sense." I frown as I lift my box off the floor. "This is crazy heavy now. I can't carry any more than this."

"That's fine. I'll just stick these papers and that bag of jerky in my box and we'll go."

Someone clears their throat from behind us. "Greggory, I'm glad you came in. I feel terrible about this, but company policy left my hands tied. I'm sorry."

Greggory stops shuffling things in his box and looks at, I assume, his old boss. "Mr. Fronze, I am sorry to have disgraced this company."

"Little choices can have big consequences. Was it worth it?"

Greggory's eyes harden defensively. "It wasn't for me, and

believe it or not, it saved a life that matters very much to me, so I don't regret it."

Mr. Fronze looks Greggory in the eye like he wants to believe him and sticks out his hand. "I know you will find something better somewhere else. Good luck."

Greggory takes the man's hand and shakes it firmly. "Thanks, boss." The man walks away, and I see regret fill my brother's eyes as he watches him go.

I tug on Greggory's shirt. "Don't get all sentimental on me. We have a job to do right now."

Greggory seems to come to himself. "Right. Of course. Follow me." I trail him as he takes me around a corner into another big room with big machines and only one person operating all of them. One wall of the room has a gigantic window; it kind of reminds me of the school room in the glass dorm except there is a giant desk on the other side of the window and two men sitting there talking to each other and an unseen audience. Greggory smiles at the short, dark-haired man running the machines. "Hey, Victor, Winifred said there was something for you at the front desk."

"Really? I wonder what it is."

"Go get it. I'll watch the live-feed for you while you're gone."

"I don't think I'm supposed to do that."

"Five minutes isn't going to hurt anything. I think your

mom might have dropped off your dinner or something. It smelled tasty."

"Hmm. All right. Don't touch anything. I have everything the way I need it for the night."

"No problem."

As soon as Victor leaves the live-feed room, Greggory locks the door and shoves a chair underneath the handle. He calls out to me, "Set those boxes by the window over there. We'll grab what we can before we leave." I nod wordlessly and obey.

Greggory whips the small video tape out of his pocket and leads me to a big black machine in the center of the room. I see a small screen on the side of it that shows the two men behind the giant desk. A little timer is counting down from 30:00 in the corner. I guess that the 27:44 I see means there are 27 minutes left in this news broadcast.

Greggory opens a slot in the big machine and sticks the little tape in quicker than a wink. With the push of a button, the news broadcasters turn into the laundry room in the complex. I feel the breath leave my body. I see Dahlia, who used to be so cheerful as she did her work, shoving heavily soiled clothes into a big, black washing machine like a zombie. Everyone else around her has the same blank stare as they labor like robots. The timer in the corner now says 14:35. Can we keep everyone out of this room for 15 minutes? The men on the other side of the window just keep talking like everything is normal.

147

Bam, bam, bam. "Hey, Greggory, let me in," Victor calls through the tiny window in the door. "Those cinnamon rolls aren't for me, they are for everyone. Winifred said you brought them in."

Greggory doesn't open the door but talks through the tiny window in it. "Yeah, I did, man. Go get seconds."

"She won't let me."

"Yes, she will. I wanted you to have more than the rest." My attention keeps splitting between Victor and the little screen that shows 10-year-olds pouring scalding-hot, liquid metal into various molds. The timer says 11:18 minutes left.

"I'll try."

"Good man, Victor." Greggory's smile melts off his face as he turns to me. "The sweet rolls will keep people busy for a little while, but we'll have to get out of here soon. Almost everyone is eating up front right now, but somebody will notice what's on the air eventually. Take a look at the outside window and figure out how we're going to escape when they try to break the door down."

I nod and run to the window. It unlatches easily, and I push the pane all the way up. It's bigger than the laundry chute that Avra and I escaped the complex through. There is a thick black screen covering the opening though. I punch it with my fist, hoping it will rip. It doesn't, my fist bounces back at me in an awkward way. I start scanning the desks around the room for scissors.

Bam, bam, bam. "Greggory, the boss said I have to get back in here. Let me in, man."

"No, Victor. I can't do that. I have to do something."

"What are you doing?"

"I'm showing people what happens every day in the Complex of Undesirables."

"What? You're going to get fired, man."

Greggory smiles through the window. "I'm already fired."

"What? You tricked me. Let me in!"

"No, sorry, man."

"I'm going to get Mr. Fronze."

My brother yells across the room, "Elira! Where is the tape at?"

I run to the little screen on the big machine. "It's the death doctor. He just gave a little kid a lethal injection. It says 6:55."

"Good. Five more minutes, and all the good stuff will have been seen."

Bam, bam, bam. "Greggory, open this door right now," his old boss commands.

"No, sir. I'm trying to make the world a better place for everyone."

"You will be put in solitary for this. Open the door now!" When Greggory quits responding, his old boss calls to Victor, "Call the peace officers. Tell them we have an emergency!"

Greggory's eyes are frantic. "Elira, where is the video now?"

"Henry Ricks just threw a couple of body bags in an unmarked grave. It shows 4:22 on the timer."

"Okay. I think we better go." My brother's voice is overtaken by the sound of something heavy hitting the door. It sounds like a mallet or maybe a small desk. The news anchors quit talking and are looking at us like they don't know what to do.

I give up on scissors and grab a pen to stab the window screen with. I rip a tiny hole with the pen and pull with all my might to make the hole bigger, big enough for us to get out. I grab the two picture frames from the box and jump out the window. When I look back, Greggory is hugging his bag of jerky and looking at me with eyes full of fear. "Come on! It's five feet down; It won't break your toes. Let's go!" The door to the live-feed room bursts open, and Greggory suddenly finds the motivation to fling himself through the window.

We sprint as fast as we can to Greggory's blue car. Peace officer cars with their lights blaring pull into both of the parking lot entrances to block the way as we reach the car. "Greggory! Get us out of here!"

My brother whips out of his parking space, swerves around a peace officer, plows over the landscaping rock and bushes, and flies onto the road. He takes off like the building is crashing down around us, but so does one of the peace officers. He is hot on our trail.

Chapter 19

GREGGORY STARTS OFF on the main road, but as
soon as he gets the chance to turn off onto a country road, he
does. The peace officer just follows us. Since that didn't work,
we turn sharply to get back on the main road a few minutes
later. The peace officer almost flips his car, but he stays on
our trail. I lean over to check the speedometer. Greggory is
going over 100 miles an hour. I have never gone this fast. "Um,
Greggory, what if someone pulls out in front of us?" He doesn't
answer me. This feels incredibly dangerous. I see the lights of
Herrington ahead and when we reach them, he slows down

slightly and starts turning in and out of little streets. "I'm scared, Greggory. What are we going to do?"

My brother's face is serious. "I thought this might happen. I know of an old-fashioned car wash that no one ever uses anymore. If I can lose this guy for a minute, I'll pull into there and take you to a secret basement room there where girls and I used to go and—talk."

I'm so nervous, I don't fully comprehend what he's saying. "Okay. I'm so glad you have a plan."

It's around 8:15 in the evening and it's getting dark. We turn down a road in the older part of town. Greggory turns off his headlights, which startles a gasp out of me. "Can you see where you're going?"

"Yeah, no sweat. I know this place like the back of my hand." We pull into an old building with long, black plastic strips hanging in the garage door. I guess this is the car wash that no one uses anymore?

Greggory turns off the car and opens his door. "Be quiet as a mouse and follow me." I shut my door as softly as I can and follow my brother to some dark, creepy-looking steps. When we get to the bottom, Greggory has to use his shoulder to get the old, rusty-hinged door to open.

Darkness and spider webs greet us. I jump as a long string of web lands in my hair. "There is a light switch here somewhere." My brother feels along the wall until he finds it. A dim light bulb hanging from the center of the room gives us just enough light to take in our surroundings. The room that opens up to us is dusty, spider webby, and full of old, mismatched furniture. The rickety wooden table to the right is covered in dusty, glass bottles.

Greggory chuckles to himself. "It looks exactly the same as we left it after our graduation party."

"Who's we?"

"My friend Jack and I used to hang out here all the time. His parents own this place. We'd bring girls, snacks, and—beverages down here after school. His parents didn't care. It looks like they still don't care. We'll be safe here."

I shudder as I look at the footprints my feet left in the dust. "How long should we wait before we go home?"

My brother doesn't look me in the eyes. "Uh, I'm a little bit worried that my bad publicity just got worse. I'll probably have to camp out here for a while."

I wish we had thought this through before now. "What about me? Garth is expecting me. Mom is too, for that matter."

He puts a hand on each of my shoulders. "I bet their house will be swarming with peace officers tonight. We better just spend the night here." He feels my shoulders slump. "I'm sorry, sis. If I hadn't been fired, it would have taken longer for them to realize that it was me who did it."

I sigh as I notice a queen-sized bed in the corner of the room. It's covered in dust, but it looks comfortable enough. "I call the open side of the bed."

"You can have the whole thing. I'll sleep on the couch." Greggory hurries to the bed and pulls off the covers and sheets, revealing a discolored mattress underneath. "I—uh, I mean, you—uh, don't want to sleep on this bedding."

I feel my frustration rising to the surface. "I don't want to sit at the table covered in an inch of dust and beer bottles either, but what choice do I have? This is the ghost of your party days; no surface is clean in here."

My brother takes my hand and forces me to look at him. "Hey, let's take a step back and be thankful that the peace officer didn't just get us. You were this close to going back to the complex tonight." He shows me a tiny space between his thumb and pointer finger. "This used to be a place of—unsavory things, but if we clean it up, it can be quite cozy."

I take a deep breath and let it out. "Is there anything we can clean with, so I can at least sit down without dust sticking to me?"

Greggory nods. "This is a car wash. I'm sure there is a box or two of soap and rags around here somewhere." He walks over to a corner filled with boxes, and rips a few open. "See! Rags, sponges, drop cloths, and what do you know? Gallons of spot-free rinse! If it can get bug guts off cars, it can get dust and grime off things too."

I pull an industrial-sized garbage can to the table and sweep all of the empty glass bottles into it. The clanging and breaking of glass is louder than I expected it to be. "Oops."

Greggory stops my hand from reaching more bottles. "We better keep it quiet. That peace officer will be scouring the neighborhood for a while, I'm sure."

"You're right. Sorry." I place the rest of the bottles into the garbage can one by one. "I'm really thirsty. Is it okay if we open that case of bottled water over there?"

"Go for it. Jack's parents have probably forgotten that this storage room even exists."

I smile for the first time in hours. "Perfect." I rip a bottle of water out of its packaging and guzzle half of it down. It really doesn't taste too bad. I pour the other half of the bottle onto a car-wash-sized rag and sponge. The gallon jug of car soap takes some muscle to open, but I drizzle a little bit of that onto the sponge too. I wash the table and hard wooden chairs down so there isn't a speck of dust or dried-on alcohol anywhere. I move on to the old-fashioned fridge, television, and rocking chair after that.

Greggory has pulled everything off the bed and removed a nasty looking blanket off the couch. "I am going to cover all the soft surfaces with those white drop cloths, and I have a blanket in the back of my car. I'll go get it."

My brother is a pretty resourceful guy. When he comes back, I ask, "Why do you keep a blanket in the back of your car?"

"You never know when you might—need it."

"Do you think this old television works?" I ask as I wipe it off.

"Yeah, at least it did three years ago."

I twist an old-fashioned dial from 'off' to 'on'; the screen lights up, but there's no sound and it's all fuzzy. I fidget with the buttons and knobs until I get the national news station; it must be the one station everyone gets, no matter how poor or old-fashioned they are. I am not surprised to see Greggory's face on the screen. I turn up the volume to hear what they are saying about him.

The news reporter looks distressed. "The interruption in our regular broadcast tonight was perpetrated by this man, a former employee of this news station, Greggory Hamble, who is also the drug addict brother of our newly elected senator, Brock Hamble. John, does all of this seem like a coincidence to you?"

Greggory places two white drop cloths on the dusty couch, so we can sit down as we watch. "No, Phil. I don't think this is a coincidence. Brock Hamble wins his election by the skin of his teeth yesterday, gets sworn in this morning, and tonight his brother, Greggory, puts a video of never-before-seen footage of the inside of the Complex of Undesirables on national news as he is cleaning out his desk. That doesn't seem like a coincidence at all. What about the teenage girl who helped Greggory? Do you have a picture of her? I believe we do, Phil. Yes, here she is. The receptionist said that Hamble claimed she was his cousin,

Edith. We have an investigative reporter looking into her. I guess the question is, did Greggory Hamble do this on his own, or is the whole Hamble family plotting something? They did lose a daughter, Elira, to the complex 14 years ago, and she is one of the complex escapees from—wait a minute, Phil, can we bring the picture of Greggory Hamble's accomplice back up? Yes. Here she is, John. You know, she kind of looks like the rest of the Hambles; I'm just going to voice this out loud without thinking about it too much first. Is it possible that the young woman we are looking at is in fact—Elira Hamble, the complex escapee?" The news anchors go silent for a moment; so do Greggory and I.

Greggory pounds a fist onto the arm of the sofa. "This is just great. I don't think we'll be able to go home anytime soon, Elira."

My longing for Garth and Avra is not going to be satisfied tonight. I have calmed down enough to realize what needs to happen. "I guess we should just stay here for a while. I just hope everyone is in the bunker before the peace officers take over our house."

My brother's eyes look far away. "Poor Avra. She can't even walk yet. Now she's going to be trapped in that dark room for who knows how long."

I jump to my feet. "We only have minutes before our parents are under constant surveillance. Is there any way to call them and tell them we're safe and secure?"

157

Greggory scratches the back of his head in an agitated way. "Yeah. Well, maybe. There used to be an ancient telephone in the roll-top desk over there. If they are still paying the power bill on this place, they might be paying the telephone bill too."

We rush to the little desk and roll the top up. An olive-green telephone with a huge dial full of holes under the receiver looks back at us. I pick the receiver up and listen for a dial-tone. Nothing but silence fills my ear. "Oh no. It doesn't work."

Greggory picks the telephone up and points to the bottom of it. "No cords. It isn't plugged into the wall. Do you see a cord anywhere?"

I frantically stack all the books and papers scattered on the desk into a neat pile on the rocking chair that I just cleaned. When I pick up a spiral-bound notebook that has 'Greggory Hamble, English,' scrawled on the front of it, I find a gray cord wound into a bundle underneath it. "Here's a cord!"

"Yes. This is a phone cord." Greggory plugs one end of the cord into the ancient phone and then traces his hand along the wall behind the desk until he finds a small square hole in it. I hold the receiver to my ear, praying that I'll hear something soon. As soon as he plugs the cord into the wall, I hear a dial tone.

I jump up and down. "Greggory! It works! Help me call home."

"You're lucky that I'm so full of useless information, Elira. Stick your finger in the hole on the dial of the number you want and spin your finger clockwise until it won't go any farther. Pull your finger out once that happens; the dial will spin back to where it started. Then do it again for the next digit in the phone number."

"Okay." My finger shakes as I dial. Greggory places his hand over mine so I don't mess up. Somehow, I get it right on the first try. I hear the phone on the other end ringing.

"Hello?" My mother's voice reveals that has been crying.

I wonder if the peace officers are already there. "Mrs. Hamble, are there extra eyes and ears with you?"

"No. Elira, where are you? Garth said you went with Greggory, and now I'm watching the two of you on the news. Our cover is blown. Two peace officers just pulled up to the house, and I don't think they'll leave anytime soon. Your friends can't leave the bunker, and you better not come home. Are you safe?"

"Yes, Greggory and I are hiding in the storage room of an old car wash. We're safe and secure." I hear a *ding dong* in the background. Our privacy has just ended for who knows how long.

"I love you both. Good job getting the video on the air. Don't come home; I'll get a hold of you again when it's safe. Take care of yourselves. Bye."

"Bye, Mom. I love you." *Click.*

I turn to look at my brother. "The peace officers arrived as we were talking. What will they do to them?"

Greggory takes the phone out of my shaking hand and hangs it up. He leads me to the couch and sits me next to him. "They'll be interrogated, but the peace officers won't hurt them. They'll figure out the truth about you whether Mom and Dad talk or not."

"Dad's hands are still healing from the last dumb thing I did. Are you sure they won't hurt him?"

Greggory shakes his head. "They'll be fined and watched 24/7."

"What about my friends?"

"They will have to live in the bunker now. I just hope they have a bucket in there to pee in."

I cover my face with my hands. "It wasn't supposed to turn out like this. We were hiding so well."

Greggory's eyebrows crease with frustration. "I know. I'm sorry. It seems like my fault. First the picture of me buying…"

"What we needed to save Avra's life."

He throws his hands in the air. "And then I get fired right as I need people to trust me at the news station."

I shake my head. "It's not your fault; we needed the sheol."

"I shouldn't have taken you with me. Now everyone knows your secret, and Mom and Dad are going to be watched and fined as accomplices to your breakout."

I lean back on the sofa in defeat. "It's like all of our hands got tied at the exact same time. I hope Brock is still able to move things forward alone. I kind of doubt he will do anything without us whispering in his ear though."

Greggory shrugs. "Yeah. He is just the smiling face of this rebellion, after all."

I feel a tear slide down my cheek. I wipe it away before any more can join it. "If we have to live here, I want the floor clean. If you sweep, I'll scrub it with sponges."

"Okay. Deal."

Wetness. My hands and knees are wet with soapy water, my armpits are wet with sweat, and my cheeks are wet with tears. I wish I could enjoy the wetness of a shower when I'm done, but there isn't one in this storage room. I just want to go home to my beautiful shower and soft bed, but I push that thought to the back of my mind as I scrub the nastiness off the floor. "What's in the fridge, Greggory?"

"You don't want to know. I'm throwing all of it away. At least it's cold. I'll scrub it down once I have it empty."

"Thank you."

"You're probably hungry. I'll bring in the bag of jerky from the car. I'll grab it when I'm done."

"Bring the pictures of our family too."

Greggory squeezes my shoulder as he walks past me to the garbage can. "Okay. They will make this place feel a little bit more like home."

Once the floor shines, I collapse onto the couch. My body hurts and my only clothes are wet and dirty. It's going to be a long night. At least my hands are clean—and wrinkly. Greggory walks back in and plops down on the couch with me. He has a bundle of stuff in his arms. He throws the bag of jerky he brought from the news station at me. I dig into it gratefully. He sets the two pictures of our family on the little side table by the couch. I'm glad I cleaned it off. He looks at me with a smirk on his face as he pulls plastic covers off two royal blue jumpsuits.

"I know this isn't your first choice of apparel, but they're clean and dry. I found them in a closet upstairs."

I start to laugh in a tired and irrational way. "Why not? I'm going to call this the 'backwards freedom day.' I may as well put on a jumpsuit again."

Greggory looks distressed. "If you sleep in wet clothes, you'll get sick, and Dad isn't here to help you."

I start to cry. "I know. I wish he was here. I wish Mom and Garth were here too."

Greggory sets the jumpsuits down and wraps his arm around me. "I know I'm a poor second or third choice, but I'm here."

I wipe my eyes with my hand and smile. "Thank you, Greggory."

"Get into some dry clothes and let's get some sleep. I'm sure everything will seem better in the morning."

I roll my eyes. "Do you really believe that?"

"Mom used to tell me that, and honestly, things do seem better when my sleep tank is full."

"But what about toothpaste and breakfast and…"

"Shh. We'll worry about it in the morning."

Chapter 20

"ELIRA, WAKE UP," my brother's voice whispers in my ear.

I moan as my body screams at me from the deep cleaning last night. "Why? There's nothing to eat. And no shower to take. And no Garth."

Greggory's voice is surprisingly cheerful. "Actually, I made a quick trip to the grocery store while you were sleeping, and I brought back muffins and juice!"

"Really?" I jump out of bed, excited beyond belief for the simple food I'm about to eat. I sit down at the table and dig into a lemon poppyseed muffin. "Thank you, Greggory. You really shouldn't have though. They probably recognized you."

My brother turns on the old television and sits down on the couch to watch it. "It's amazing how little people looked at me when I was wearing this jumpsuit. I was just a grunt worker to them. Well, except one elderly woman. She, uh, winked at me."

I giggle. "You should call yourself 'the invisible man—with a flirtatious grandma weakness.'"

Greggory takes off his shoes and throws one of them at me. "Gross."

I dodge in the nick of time. "Ha, ha!"

My brother's eyes light up as he watches the television screen. "Uh, Elira, come here. Bring your breakfast."

I grab a bottle of orange juice and a second muffin before I join my brother on the couch. "What's going on? Why are all of those people shouting?"

Greggory claps his hands together. "People are rioting! They are disgusted by what is going on in the complex. The video is working after all!

"No way," I say as I shove a big chunk of muffin in my mouth. "Where is this protest happening?" I ask with full cheeks.

He points to the screen. "The Herrington City Building, which is perfect. A mob at the entrance there is going to be hard to ignore."

I take in my drab surroundings. "How far away is that from here?"

"Only four blocks." I see a gleam in my brother's eye as he asks, "Why? Do you want to go?"

I don't have parents calling the shots anymore. Is this a stupid idea? "Yes, I want to go! This is what we've been working for. If enough people are upset, they'll have to listen to Brock when he proposes to change the law. How many people do you think are there?"

Greggory cringes as he pulls off his stinky socks. "I don't know, 100 probably."

"That's not amazing, but it's a start. We should go in our normal clothes. I think a guy and a girl in jumpsuits will draw attention considering the video they are protesting."

Greggory unzips his jumpsuit and changes right in front of me. "What should we do about your eye?"

"Geez, Greggory! You should warn me to turn around at least."

"Sorry. I forget how—innocent you are."

I roll my eyes. "There are worse things to be. I've been trying not to rub my eye. Is the makeup gone?"

"Well, no, it's not gone, but a little bit of purple is showing through on the side of your face. Just keep your hair over that eye and you'll be fine."

"Okay. I'm going to change; would you please turn around?"

Greggory snorts. "Yes." He looks around the room. "Actually, I think I'll make a wall for us to change behind with those boxes in the corner."

I cautiously unzip my jumpsuit. "Good idea. You were right, by the way."

He starts moving boxes around. "Right about what?"

"I do feel better now that my sleep tank is full."

He sets a box at eye level on the wall he's making. "Ha! I told you. It works for me every time."

I pull my shirt over my head and straighten it out as best I can. "Okay, I'm ready. Are there any hats or glasses laying around here?"

Greggory puts the last row of boxes almost to the ceiling. "Yeah, there were some company hats and jackets in the closet upstairs. I think there was a pair of sunglasses too. Let's go join a protest."

I DEFINITELY APPRECIATE all the conveniences of my parents' house as we dig around the dusty little closet in the upstairs office of the car wash. I brush the dust off a Sparkly Clean Car Wash baseball cap and jacket before I put them on. The sunglasses we find are not particularly feminine, but they're better than nothing. Greggory pulls his expensive-looking sunglasses out of his car for himself.

He looks at mine and then at his. "Do you want to trade glasses?" he asks.

I shrug. "Nah, it's fine. Yours suit you."

He smiles and slides his glasses on. "Okay. I think we should walk. The peace officers are probably looking for my car."

The dust we've stirred up makes me cough. "Yeah, I need some fresh air anyway."

We walk down the quiet, older part of town without seeing any peace officers or pedestrians at all. Greggory points to the biggest house on the street. "That's my friend Jack's parents' house. They are the only people with money left on this side of town."

"Should we talk to them about staying in the car wash? Or will they turn us in?"

Greggory rubs his chin. "I don't know. I think we should play it on the safe side. If they find us, I'll talk to them, but I'm not going to seek them out."

We turn the corner and are amazed at the noise and scene that greet us. There are definitely more than 100 people here. I'd say it's closer to 1,000. People are yelling and holding signs that say things like, 'Stop Tearing Our Families Apart,' and, 'Complex=Slavery and Death.'

I see a familiar-looking pregnant woman leading the front of the crowd in a chant. "Every human has a flaw! Repeal the Complex Law!" the people yell.

My heart swells with pride as I watch Molly trying to save her unborn baby and convincing others to join her cause. I join in with the chanting as I watch the doors and windows of the city building. Is anyone going to come out and address the crowd?

A woman keeps turning around and looking at me. She doesn't say anything, but I wonder if she recognizes me. She turns her attention to Greggory after a while. I feel like I should talk to her before she talks to anyone else. I sidle up next to her and say in her ear so she can hear me over the crowd, "Do you know me? You keep looking at my friend and me."

The woman looks closely at my face, particularly the left-side of my face. "Are you the Hambles who put the complex video on the air yesterday?"

Oh, no. What should I say? I smile sweetly at her. "What would you do if we were?"

She smiles with excitement. "I would probably hug you. I've been dying inside since they took my son away eight years ago. No one has taken my side when I've said how cruel and unfair the law is until now. So, tell me the truth. Are you the Hambles?"

I think I can trust her. "Well, this is Greggory Hamble, but I'm just..."

"Elira Hamble."

Oh, boy. I narrow my eyes at her. "You can't believe everything news reporters guess at."

She leans forward. "Oh, haven't you seen the news this morning? Investigators couldn't find a birth certificate for Edith Westergard. Your parents even confirmed that Edith Westergard doesn't exist after some careful interrogation. Everyone knows that you're Elira Hamble."

I feel my stomach drop. Why did I venture out into this crowd today? Everyone knows that I am wanted for two things now. The bounty on my head has got to be enormous. I lean closer to her. "Are you going to turn me in?"

She scoffs at me. "No. I want to help you. Things are finally changing because of you." She pulls some cash out of her pocket. "Here, take this money. Use it however you need to; living in hiding must be hard. Your makeup is coming off your birthmark, too, by the way. Buy more of that." I pocket the money as she leans in closer. "Rumors are circulating around the crowd that we will probably have to move our protest to the capital city. You'll need money to travel that far."

I have to speak louder as the roaring crowd starts a new chant. "I don't know what to say. Thank you. I don't even know your name."

"Laura. Laura Beckman. My son's name is William Beckman. Help me get him out. I live in the only red house on Pine Street. If you need my help in any way, don't hesitate to ask me."

It's a good thing the boisterous crowd is watching Molly up front because I wrap my arms around the total stranger in appreciation. I whisper in her ear, "Laura, I appreciate this so much. I have a question though. How safe do you think I am? Do these people think like you, or do you think they'll turn me in for the bounty? What is my bounty at now?" I take a step back to watch her face.

Laura looks around the loud crowd. She has to raise her voice to be heard. "These people think like me; I mean, look at them chanting." She lowers her voice and leans into my ear. "You could probably wipe the makeup completely off your eye and they'd lift you on their shoulders like a hero. But I'd be careful in public in general. Especially around people who haven't been negatively affected by the Complex Law. The bounty on your head is at $80,000. Greggory and the rest of your friends' bounties are at $20,000."

My eyes grow huge. "Yikes! That's good to know. Thank you."

Greggory nudges me. "I think I see Damon writing on a notebook over there."

I squint my eyes to see the man in a black hooded sweatshirt better. "That's not Damon, that's a hoodlum."

My brother laughs. "He obviously doesn't want everyone to know who he is. Let's go talk to him."

"Okay."

We walk to the edge of the crowd where Damon is in fact dressed like a hoodlum and is taking notes. He raises his eyes briefly as we approach him. He does a double-take when he sees me. "Elira!" he says as he drops his notebook and wraps his arms around me. He whispers in my ear, "I've been so worried about you. You thought you pissed the government off when you escaped. Ha! They will kill you if they find you now."

I look at him questioningly. "What's changed? I went from being a wanted woman to—a wanted woman?"

Damon taps my forehead with his pen. "Your video has the country in an outrage! Brock's secretary says the phones have not stopped ringing all morning, and there is a line circling the building to see him. People want the Complex Law changed after all!"

I smile at Damon as I let that news sink in. "I knew they would. It's time to reunite families."

Damon's focus goes from me to the city building in the blink of an eye. "Hey, look! Someone is coming to the door. It looks like the new mayor of Herrington, Johnathan Lawrence."

The overweight, balding man that is approaching the crowd wipes his considerable forehead with a handkerchief before addressing us. The crowd hushes so they can hear him without a microphone. "Hello, my fellow city members. I know you have all been outraged by the film that was leaked on the news last night showing the inside of the Complex of Undesirables. Very few people know for sure what goes on in there. This video probably doesn't portray the true day-to-day activity that has benefited our society for 150 years. We do have people of lesser abilities making goods for the community in a helpful way there after all."

The crowd erupts. "BOO! DEPRAVITY! SLAVERY! DEATH! BRING DOWN THE COMPLEX!"

Mayor Lawrence wipes his forehead again. "Now, now. If you wish to make a change to the Complex Law that has successfully improved our country all these years, you'll have to take your complaints to the senators and President Prystine in the capital city. We only have limited power here. I can only change Herrington laws."

A loud man who looks an awful lot like Scott's dad shouts, "When is the high-speed monorail to Adanlay opening to the public?"

"Next Monday."

Molly walks in front of the mayor and speaks into a megaphone that someone in the crowd hands her. "We will march on the capital city next Monday. We will fill the monorail with protestors all morning long and start our protest march at the capital building at noon sharp. Are you with me?"

"YEAH!" the crowd shouts back.

The mayor looks confused and cowed as he backs up and eventually retreats inside the city building again. Damon scribbles away in his notebook. A scruffy-looking man steps up to me and says, "Edith, I don't think you should be this exposed. Do you see the peace officers lining the city building? They will snatch you up in a heartbeat."

I don't look at the man as I ask, "How do you know who I am?"

He leans in closer and whispers in a voice less deep, "Because I'm Ernestine."

I throw my arms around my disguised friend. "Is everyone okay?"

"Get off me! Yes. They are fine for now. There is a peace officer inside your parents' house 24/7 and another outside."

"Oh, no. How did you get out?"

"I know how to climb through windows and scale buildings. I was fine. The rest of your friends are going to have cabin fever before long, though. They can't leave the bunker. Not to shower or go to the bathroom, not at all, unless the peace officer leaves."

"Someone should draw him out every so often."

"Yeah, I am thinking of ways to do that. Don't worry about us. We'll figure it out. Where are the two of you hiding?"

I plop my hand on top of my head. "Have you read my hat?"

Ernestine squints as she reads, "Sparkly Clean Car Wash. Isn't that place abandoned?"

Greggory leans toward Ernestine's ear. "Yep. We have it all to ourselves. We're actually in the basement storage room."

"Good. I'll stop by when I have news. Here is some money. Your parents are going to be worried sick until you're back under their roof."

I add the bills to the ones the kind lady gave me. "I know, my mom is probably furious at me for lying about where I was going last night. Don't let her worry about us. Greggory is resourceful on the street, and I have two new friends who want to help us."

Ernestine looks at me suspiciously. "Who?"

Damon has been standing back a few steps, but he steps forward and shakes Ernestine's hand. I whisper into her ear, "This is Damon from Brock's campaign; you should remember him from voting day, and my other friend is Laura, that woman over there in the red shirt."

Ernestine nods at Damon and then looks in the direction I'm pointing. "I think I recognize her. She had a son taken away a while ago, right?"

"Yes."

"Perfect. You can trust parents of complex kids. This protesting is great. I think the government officials are scratching their heads today."

Damon asks Ernestine, "Are you going to the protest in Adanlay on Monday?"

She adjusts the fake beard on her face. "If I can, yes."

I butt in. "Good. I don't know if Greggory and I should risk it."

Ernestine shakes her head. "Don't go. You two are worth a lot of money; you need to watch your backs. Do you have any messages you want me to take back to the house?"

I nod energetically. "Tell Avra I'm sorry I can't come home to help her, and tell Garth that I love him." Damon frowns and turns around with his notebook.

Ernestine rolls her manly-looking eyes. "Do you want to say anything to your parents?"

I feel my cheeks redden with embarrassment. "Oh, yeah. Tell them that I'm safe and happy, and I love them too."

Ernestine looks at the peace officers that are moving closer to the crowd. "Will do, kid. I'll see you later."

"Bye, Ernestine."

I AM SO FULL OF JOY as my brother and I walk back to our hideout. "Did you see how many people were there? That crowd cares about people like me, Greggory!"

He smirks at me. "It's nice to have you feeling comfortable in a crowd. I was afraid you'd ask to hold my hand again." He laughs as he remembers my apprehension at the fair.

I slap his arm playfully. "Oh, shut up. I have some money. We should stop somewhere to get food and clothes."

He nods his head. "I bought us a few days' worth of food at the grocery store this morning, but we should get you some eye makeup and both of us some clothes."

"Is there anything close by?"

Greggory looks up and down the street. "Nothing fancy.

There is a variety store around the corner. It won't have much selection, but they'll have what we need there."

"Do they have a bathroom? I feel like I'm going to burst. Oh—and makeup too?"

My brother grins at me. "Yeah, they have it all."

After relieving myself, we pick out some plain colored shirts, pants, underwear, and socks in the variety store. I get a bottle of makeup that doesn't match my skin tone as well as the stuff my mother bought, but it will still work if I pull my hair in front of my eye. My brother's stomach growls as we leave the store. "Have you ever had pizza, Elira?"

"Peet seh? I don't think so. It must not be one of Chef Freda's specialties."

Greggory snorts. "Oh, I'm sure she could make a fine pizza if she wanted to. Mom and Dad just have a more refined palate than the rest of us."

"Do they sell it around here?"

He points straight ahead. "Yeah, that little shop on the end there sells it by the slice during lunch time. Do you want to try it?"

"Sure."

We set our shopping bags down at a little table in the tiny dining room of Toto's Pizzeria. My brother directs me to a glass and metal contraption covered in delicious looking circles. I pick out a slice covered in meats and another one covered in vegetables. I feel my mouth water as I wonder which one I'll like the best. Greggory picks one slice covered in ham and pineapple and another covered in chicken and spinach. He pays the owner from his own wallet. No one bothers us as we sit down and eat. I really like both of my flavors. The meat one is especially good, but then I try a bite of each of Greggory's slices and I change my mind. The chicken one positively sings in my mouth. I give my brother a thumbs up sign as I chew it.

As we pick up our shopping bags and head to the door, the old man behind the counter says, "You two be careful out there, okay. If you ever need something, you come talk to your Uncle Toto."

Greggory nods at the man. "We will. Thank you, my friend."

I smile at the old man and whisper to my brother as we leave. "Do you know him?"

He nods. "Jack and I used to get pizza here all the time. He remembers me."

"Will he turn us in?"

My brother looks back at the pizzeria. "Nah. He has secrets of his own, and he values loyal customers."

"Good."

Chapter 21

WHEN WE GET BACK to our secret bungalow, Greggory adds another layer of boxes to the wall that we will use for our changing room. I organize the clutter pushed around the sides of the room and wash down anything I missed yesterday.

"Do you want to use these for our new clothes?"

Greggory looks into the box I hand him. "Yeah."

Greggory rummages through the old box of hangers I find, and hangs our new clothes on the wall of cardboard boxes. He's probably used to having a walk-in closet. I do a quick check of all the food we have. Greggory did well choosing foods that don't have to be cooked. I'm just concerned about how we're going to handle the showering and going to the bathroom part of life.

When I ask Greggory about that, he says, "There is a half bathroom upstairs that the employees of the car wash used to use. I tried it this morning. The toilet and sink still work."

I light up with this news. "That's a relief. I'm sure it needs a good cleaning though."

Greggory shudders. "Yeah, it's just as bad as this room was last night."

I imagine shoving my arms and legs in the sink. "How will we bathe or shower?"

My brother scratches his head. "Well, this is a car wash, surely we can wash our bodies here too." He snaps his fingers. "We can either use the high-power sprayer or fill the giant soaker solution bucket with hot water for a bath. Which would you prefer?"

I imagine trying to spray myself, or worse yet, my brother spraying me, while I'm naked, with a high-power sprayer. "I'll probably go for the giant bucket bath. I'll go clean the bathroom first. Will you fill the bucket with hot water for me afterward?"

Greggory shrugs. "Yeah. I'll leave it outside the bathroom door."

"Are there any better cleaning supplies up there?"

"Yeah, tons. I'll show you."

Greggory opens a cupboard by the bathroom door to

reveal soaps, scrub brushes, rags, towels, small buckets, and something called a squeegee. He shows me how to use the squeegee to basically scrape water off of windows. He decides to wash his car while I scrub down the bathroom.

The half bathroom is surprisingly big and disgustingly dirty. It's tiled floor to ceiling and there is a huge drain in one corner. I decide to hurl a small bucket of soapy water all over the walls, sink, and toilet and let it soak before I start scrubbing. It's weird, but I'm actually thankful for the time I had to scrub the bathroom in the glass dorm for job research weeks now that I have to do this. I am surprised to see that the bathroom tile is white instead of brown after I get the years of grime off everything. It kind of reminds me of the white bathroom in the glass dorm once it's clean and sparkling.

I open the door to the bathroom to find a huge black bucket full of hot water waiting for me. I try to drag it into the bathroom by myself but it's too heavy. Greggory sees me struggling and helps me by pushing the bucket through the door. Once it's in the corner I can close the door behind me. The dim light bulb hanging above my head doesn't let me see every detail of the bucket, but it looks like Greggory scrubbed it down before he filled it with water. I take off my clothes and sink down until I'm sitting on the bottom of the giant make-shift tub. My head and knees are sticking out, but the rest of me is covered in hot water. Ahh. It feels so good. I could almost fall asleep. I close my eyes for just a few seconds...

Knock, Knock. What? Who's that? What's going on?

"Elira, you've been in there for over an hour. Maybe you should get out now. I would feel better if I could see where you are."

I rub my eyes with my wet hand, which doesn't help, it just makes my eyes sting. "Sorry, I fell asleep. I'll be right out." I quickly wash myself head to toe with a weird bottle of soap. The water is barely warm anymore when I climb out of the giant bucket. Once I'm dressed in my new plain clothes, I try to figure out what to do with the water. The drain is in a low spot in the corner. Should I just dump the bucket on the floor and let the water go down the drain? Why not? I stand on the toilet lid as I tip the giant bucket over. It splashes like a tidal wave at first, but the water follows the tilt of the tiled floor and goes down the drain. I use the squeegee to help the water get there. The towel I used to dry myself off with helps me mop up the remaining wet spots on the floor. That wasn't so bad. I could do that every other day.

When I get back to our basement bungalow, Greggory has a sandwich and a bag of potato chips waiting for me on the couch. The old television shows us some very unhappy-looking politicians. "You've got to see this, Elira. There were riots at every single city building in the country today. The people of the United Cities are outraged by what is going on in the complexes."

"Really? That's perfect," I say through a mouth full of chips.

"I just hope Brock can get something written up to change the law without any of us to help him."

Greggory crumples his chip bag. "He is! I'm sure they'll come back to that story in a minute. The other government officials have been condemning Brock all day because you and I supposedly started this uproar."

Wet chip flecks fly out of my mouth as I exclaim, "Were you sleepwalking last night? We definitely did start this uproar!"

Greggory doesn't look amused as he wipes potato goo off his cheek with his hand. "Don't talk with your mouth full, and don't interrupt me. The common people of the country are flocking to Brock and begging him to change the Complex Law. He said he would have a public statement at 7:00 tonight from Adanlay."

I grab Greggory's arm and look at his watch. "So, any minute now."

"Yep. Ahh, here it is."

I watch my brother exit an official-looking government building and walk to a cluster of microphones. He is less smiley than usual today; his determination is plain to see.

"Hello, my fellow citizens of the United Cities. It has been an exciting few days for me and for you. I want to thank all of you who voted for me and all of you who have stayed by my side since finding out that my sister, who has escaped the Herrington Complex of Undesirables, has also been reunited with my family and helping me with my campaign. She is the

185

one who opened my eyes to the value of people with physical flaws. I have not spent much time around people with physical flaws because the Complex Law has sent them all away to be slaves in order to make other people rich. That is not morally or ethically right as you could tell from the horrific video my siblings put on the air yesterday. I cringe to imagine my unborn son joining those poor people's ranks when he is two years old. Yes. My unborn son has a heart defect, and if the law does not change, he will be taken away from me. This fact, as well as reuniting with my sister, has helped me decide to do something about the law. In fact, I am proposing we disband the entire Complex Law. If I am successful, that would mean that your children and siblings who have been shut away in the Complex of Undesirables for who knows how long, would be released to you. That also means that your elderly parents and aunts and uncles would be released to you. That is a lot of responsibility that our citizens have never had to shoulder. Are you up to that challenge?"

An enormous crowd that we can't see from our vantage point erupts into cheers of "YES! YEAH!"

My stately brother continues, "If we disband the Complex Law, then we will also be free to leave the country. My fellow senators have let me know, in no uncertain terms, that if we disband the Complex Law, they believe you all will flee the country with your loved ones as quickly as you can." Brock pauses for emphasis as the crowd mumbles. "I have assured them that we are still proud citizens of the United Cities. We will stay together no matter what and take care of each other even with added responsibilities to citizens who have been shut away. Was I right to say that?"

"YES! YEAH!"

He smiles with confidence. "I knew I was right. We are a strong country and we want to treat everyone fairly no matter what their flaw is. If you are under the delusion that you do not have a flaw, do a quick self-evaluation; is there any physical, mental, emotional, or financial imperfection about you? We all have them. That's what makes us human and helps us try harder. Will you help me disband the Complex Law?"

"YES!"

"I knew you would. It will take your votes. Thank you all for your fine support, and God bless you all."

Wow. My brother isn't just a smiling face. He is—a leader.

Chapter 22

I WAKE UP TO THE SOUND of knocking on our hideaway door. I jump out of bed and start hyperventilating. "Greggory! Get up! They found us. I don't know how, but the peace officers found us."

My brother rolls onto his back on the couch and opens his eyes. "I doubt it. If peace officers are here, they'll just break the door down and grab us. It's probably one of our friends. Go ask."

I swallow the lump in my throat and wobble to our shabby wooden door that hides us from the rest of the world. I press my ear against it and ask, "Who's there?"

I hear a familiar, deep female voice answer back, "It's me, Ernestine. Let me in." I unlock the door and let my disguised friend in.

I am so thrilled that it's her. "What's going on? Is something wrong?"

She chuckles in her gruff way. "Well, that depends on what you call wrong. If you don't like riots, then everything is wrong, but if you're like me, then all of this dissatisfaction with the government means everything is right." Her smile is contagious.

I smile and clap my hands. "Come in and sit down. I want to know everything that is going on."

"I actually don't know a whole lot, because I'm in hiding, like you, except I don't have a television. You lucky ducks, can we turn that on?"

"Sure." Greggory turns on the television and then goes to the fridge to get us each a bowl of cereal for breakfast.

Nothing particularly exciting is airing on the national news station at the moment. I turn down the volume so we can hear each other better.

"So, how is everyone?"

"Well, Avra is walking a few steps at a time now. Scott has made it his goal to get her back to the way she was. Rocky is climbing the walls. He wants to leave the bunker with me so he can see his dad, but he just doesn't have the skill for how I've been coming in and out of the house with peace officers around 24/7."

I have a thought. "But if you could get him out once—couldn't the two of you just stay with Frank? Or is he as distasteful to you as ever?"

Ernestine looks at me like I'm a genius. "I—hadn't thought about it, but that is a good idea. I'd do anything to get out of that small, dark—We'd stay in separate rooms of course."

I smile at her. "Of course. So—how is Garth?"

Ernestine chuckles as she leans back on our old couch. "He's like a love-sick puppy dog without you."

A smile creeps onto my face. "Really?"

She grins with her crooked teeth and shakes her head. "Yeah. I have a note from him, but you can't have it until I say what I came here to say."

I slap the couch in frustration. "Oh, come on, Ernestine. Just give it to me!"

"No, I need you to focus with me for just a little bit longer. Brock has been asked to attend a meeting with the Herrington complex chief."

That is interesting. "How do you know that?"

"Well, it looks like it's the breaking news right now," Ernestine says as she points to the television. The headline blaring across the screen reads 'Senator Hamble to Meet with Herrington Complex Chief Tonight.' She leans toward me. "I knew about it late last night because your mother has been slipping notes to me through a crack on the side of the bookshelf."

"So he's going, right?"

She nods. "He is definitely going. He just really wants you to be there with him."

I laugh out loud. "I wish I could, but there's no way the complex chief would let me leave there again."

Ernestine's sly, revolutionary side surfaces. "What if you were disguised? A disguise that you've never used before."

I shake my head in defeat. "I can't get to my mother's box of tricks. I don't think I can pull it off with what I have here."

"You said yesterday that you have friends who will help you. Would they help you disguise yourself like an elderly office aide before 7:00 tonight?"

"I-I don't know, maybe. If I can't pull it off, will Brock just go to the meeting without me?"

Ernestine raises her eyebrows. "Yes. He will pick you and Damon up at 6:15 at the museum parking lot. If you aren't ready, he'll leave without you."

I pause as I consider all of my resources. "Okay, I think I can be ready by then. I will do my very best."

"That's my girl. Now you can have your letter." She pulls a white square of folded paper out of her pocket and dangles it in front of my face. I snatch the note faster than she can protect her hand from my fingernails. "Ow! You scratched me!"

"Sorry. Can I write something to him quickly, so you can take it back to him?"

Ernestine turns up the television and shrugs. "Sure."

"Thank you." I stick the note from Garth into the pocket of my jumpsuit that I'm using as pajamas, and rush to the little desk with the telephone to see what there is to write on. I find two pencils, two pens, and a long, skinny notepad that says 'Sparkly Clean Car Wash' on the top of it.

My handwriting is kind of sloppy as I hurry to put my thoughts on paper.

Dear Garth,

Can you believe what is going on? It's so exciting that our plan is working, yet sad that we're both in hiding, miles away from each other. I wish we could meet. I haven't read your note from Ernestine yet, but do you miss me at all? I miss you so much, even my toenails feel it. I'm safe and happy otherwise. Greggory and I are living in an old abandoned car wash storage room. It's comfortable enough, but I can't wait to come home. If Brock does his part, I'll be able to come home without a disguise. That kind of freedom would be delicious to me. Ernestine wants to go, so I have to end this note. I think about you every single day. I love you, Elira

Ernestine stands up and shuts off the television. "I like your little hideaway. It reminds me of my house."

I smirk as I wrap my arms around me friend. "You and

193

Rocky should definitely stay with Frank. Tell my mom and dad that I love them and give this to Garth."

"Okay, kid. Get your disguise together and help your brother stand up to the complex chief tonight, for all our sakes."

Her eyes tell me how serious this meeting is. "I will. I don't know how, but somehow, I'll do it. Thank you, Ernestine."

"Just keep telling yourself that freedom is worth it. You can do this."

Ernestine leaves and I use our new walk-in box closet to get dressed. I pull the folded piece of paper out of the jumpsuit pocket. My fingers can't open it fast enough.

Dear Elira,

I hope you're okay. I have been beating myself up about leaving you at the news station with Greggory ever since I watched the video live. The whole thing aired before they shut it off, by the way. Your mom was thrilled about that even though she was angry that you went with Greggory. She told me I couldn't drive for a month. I should have stayed to help and protect you. Now I'm not exactly sure where you are, and I'm trying not to strangle everyone in the bunker with me. I mean, I'm thankful to be safe, but Rocky can be really annoying in close quarters. Watching Scott and Avra together makes me lonely, and Ernestine's restlessness is contagious. If you were here, these four walls would feel like paradise instead of a prison. Ernestine says we may have to stay in here for months. I can't even imagine that. I might not survive. Please don't forget me. Thinking of you is the only thing that keeps me sane in here. If we last until Brock changes the Complex Law, it will be worth it. Someday, this will just be an interesting story to laugh about. I can't wait to have you back in my arms.

Write to me soon.
I love you more than anything,
Garth

My mind is going a million miles an hour as I sit at the table and smear the new makeup on my birthmark. Poor Garth. I shouldn't complain about my situation; it could be so much worse. I can at least have a bucket bath whenever I want one. I wish I had a mirror though. "Is there a mirror around here anywhere, Greggory?"

"There's the one in the bathroom upstairs. And I think I saw a broken-off side mirror from a car up there in a corner. I'll go check it out." What a nice brother.

Greggory comes back with a broken car mirror for me. Who knew that someone's broken junk would help me out so much. I'm able to smooth out my eye makeup much better now. "Do you know where Pine Street is, Greggory?"

"Yeah, it's over a mile from here. Is that where your friend is?"

"Yep. Let's walk."

He shakes his head. "Uh, no. That's a long walk and you

don't want to sweat your disguise off coming back. I'll drive. Actually, it's not far; you should drive."

That suggestion stops me in my tracks. "Aren't you tired of putting your life in your hands?"

Greggory laughs. "If I can put an illegal video on the news, I can survive a mile with you behind the wheel."

"They sound about equal on the risk scale to me."

"Whatever. Let's go."

We arrive at the only red house on Pine Street in one piece, despite my poor driving, and knock on the door. The lady from yesterday, Laura, answers it. "El—Edith, you came! Come in. How can I help you?"

After the door clicks shut, I ask quietly, "Can you disguise me like an elderly woman?"

Laura Beckman's eyebrows scrunch together for a second as she looks at me, but then she nods. "Absolutely. You came to the right house."

Chapter 23

MY NEW FRIEND has her 70-year-old mother living with her, so she happens to have everything I need, complete with a gray, curly wig. Apparently, her mom is too lazy to do her hair sometimes, so she just slips the wig on instead. My wrinkles look a tad fake to me, so I am depending on my borrowed grandma glasses to hide them.

"Laura, tell me honestly, how old do I look?"

She tilts her head as she looks at me. "I'd say late-sixties."

I take the ancient frames off my face and look at them. "Will your mother be missing her glasses?"

Laura shrugs. "Well, they are her actual glasses, but she's happy to lend them to you so she can get her grandson back."

"I will bring them back tonight when I'm done."

"Or tomorrow. Don't rush on our account."

I look at my friend appreciatively. "Your generosity is so touching. Does anything look off about me?" I turn around in a circle.

"Well, you need to walk slower and make your voice more squawky."

I hunch my back slightly and let my jaw hang open. "Okay, like thi-ss?"

She giggles. "Yeah. That's perfect." My friend looks at my brother who looks way younger than me for once. "Do you need a disguise, Greggory?"

He shakes his head dismissively. "No, I'm not going. I think having both of us in that man's office will be too risky."

Laura nods in agreement. "Okay. Elira, you know that the complex chief is going to try to talk you out of changing the law, right?"

I nod seriously. "Yeah, I know. We won't let him push us around. I hear his own staff is having a hard time watching the children work dangerous jobs. Secrecy has been his power all these years. Now that everyone knows how he's treating their family and neighbors in there, he doesn't have a leg to stand on and he knows it."

"Exactly. Don't let him fool you into thinking he has the power."

I think about that for a moment. "I won't." The clock on her kitchen wall chimes. "I better go meet Brock. Thank you for everything, Laura."

I have to remember to act old as I climb into Greggory's car, so I won't look suspicious. He laughs at me as I take forever to climb into the passenger seat. "Would Granny like to stop and get a hamburger before we meet Brock?"

I glare at him over my glasses. "You can just shut up, sonny."

BROCK IS WAITING in a fancy black car as we pull into the museum parking lot. Greggory squeezes my hand before I get out of his car. "I'll be waiting for you here at 9:00. Don't act nervous in front of him, and don't react if he threatens to do something to your friends."

It feels like ice water has just splashed me in the face. "Do you think he'll do that?"

Greggory's face is blank. "You need to go. Be strong, envision yourself leading your friends out of the complex, and you'll find a way to make it happen."

I take a deep breath and let it out. "Okay." I move slowly and stoop my back a little bit as I switch cars. Brock is the only one in the back of the car; the driver and Brock's bodyguard are in the front. My brother smiles at me. "You're looking fine today, Elira."

I glare at him over my glasses. "Everyone is a comedian today. Is anyone else coming with us?"

"Yes. My personal assistant is meeting us there and we're picking up Damon Bellvue on the way."

I remember Ernestine mentioning him. "Why Damon? Your campaign is over now; wasn't that the only thing he was hired for?"

My brother takes a long drink of some kind of weird-colored health shake. "Originally, yes. He has been on the phone with me every day the last week with some top-notch ideas. He hasn't missed a beat with what's going on in the public mind. Would you like some of my mineral shake? It keeps me awake and sharp even with no sleep."

I shudder at the color of it. "No thanks. So did you hire him permanently?"

"Yes."

I'm not sure how I feel about that. I like Damon a lot, maybe too much to be good for my relationship with Garth. I lean over and whisper to my fancy senator brother, "Do these two guys know who I really am?"

Brock finishes his shake. "Yes. I told them yesterday and they have signed a contract with me promising they won't tell anyone who you really are. So, you can trust them." Brock's bodyguard turns around and waves at me with half a smile.

I raise my eyebrows at Brock. "Okay, if you say so." We pull into the parking lot of a huge building with lots of windows and doors. I never imagined Damon to be rich enough to have a house bigger than my parents. "Wow. Damon has a huge house."

Brock looks at me and grins. "This is an apartment building. He only lives in a little section of this thing."

"Oh, I've heard of that. Maxine lives in one of these."

My brother shakes his head at me. "You crack me up. Here comes Damon."

Damon opens the door next to me, and I have to scoot over so he can slide in. He looks at me questioningly for a minute and then he starts to laugh. "What is your name today? Doris?"

Brock chuckles a little himself as he slides a name badge necklace over my head. "She's going to be Eloise, my loyal aide today. Here's one for you too, Damon. You get to keep your name."

"Thank you, I'm rather attached to it."

Brock laughs and wipes his tired-looking eyes. "Here is the game plan, you two. We will meet the complex chief in his office at the complex."

I feel like I've been blind-sided for a minute. "Wait, we have to go inside the complex for this meeting?"

Brock looks at me like this is obvious information. "Y-es. Is that going to be a problem?

I try to calm my anxiety. "No, I'll be fine." Maybe Ernestine did tell me this. I feel flustered.

Brock opens his briefcase as he continues. "Good. Anyway, I expect him to put us through a long, heroic tale of giving the 'lesser people' of the country a purpose in life and taking good care of them. We are not to believe a word of it."

"I can do that," I mumble through my teeth.

"I will demand an answer for all of the inhumanity we saw on the tape. He will try to give us a good answer which, of course, we will not believe. I will then tell him about the hundreds of people who have called, sent letters, and personally visited my office to tell me of the heartache the Complex Law has put them through."

"May I have some time to give him some statistics when he doesn't believe that people want a change?" Damon asks.

"Yes. That's why you're here."

I look from Damon's smiling face to my brother's determined one. "Why am I here?"

"To shmooze him with your good looks," Damon says with a wink.

"Stop it."

He squeezes my knee. "He's an older guy, and you're the cutest grandma I've ever seen."

I feel my cheeks turning red. "Seriously, stop it."

Brock clears his throat. "You're actually here to keep him from telling me lies. You know the complex better than any one else on my team. I may not recognize how deep the lies go."

"Okay."

Brock looks out the window and smiles at us as the car comes to a halt. "We're here." He clicks something by the handle of his briefcase.

I look at the handle curiously. "What did you just click?"

Brock smiles. "I just turned on the camera that Maxine used to incriminate the complex."

I smile so big, I can feel my makeup-covered cheeks touching my granny glasses. "Nice!"

My feet shake in my ugly shoes as I slide out of the car behind Damon. The mammoth concrete building looms above me, making me feel small and inconsequential. Why did I think I could do this? This man wants to squish me, and he can, here, in his own domain. A tall, skinny man with straight black hair and glasses joins us in front of our car. "Damon and Eloise, this is my personal assistant, Jiang. He has a photographic memory and knows the details of every law in this country inside and out. He will be a great help to us." Jiang bows his head in respect to Brock. We walk down a long sidewalk to a big door with armed complex guards on each side. I wonder if they are complex-dwellers or normal employees.

One of them speaks to us in a higher voice than we are expecting. "Hello, my name is Guard Venus. What is your business at the Complex of Undesirables today?" I cringe as I remember my last encounter with Guard Venus.

Brock looks into the black visor of her helmet and says, "We're here to meet with the complex chief by his invitation."

A deep voice comes from the other white-clad guard. "Yes, you are expected. We will have to check you for weapons." Obviously, both of these guards are employees. They must place the guards who have always lived in the complex in the back, away from the road.

Brock doesn't look enthusiastic about this. "I'm a politician and these three are my aides. Check us if you wish, but the only person who might have a weapon is my bodyguard."

The guards push Damon and me against the wall and feel up and down our bodies for weapons. I watch Damon's eyes fill with anger as the male guard's hands get near my chest. "I'm sorry, but is it necessary to manhandle a mature woman like that?"

Venus looks in Damon's briefcase, and the male guard looks in my granny purse. "You two are fine. Move aside."

Damon whispers in my ear while we watch Brock and Jiang get searched, "What a jerk. Are you okay?"

I glare at the male guard as he puts his hands all over my nicely-dressed brother. "I'm fine."

Brock's bodyguard goes last and he has to leave three guns and a knife at the door. They better give them back when we leave.

We hear an audible *click* as Guard Venus opens the door for us. Her smooth voice directs us. "Someone should be along to collect you. Walk straight ahead and take the first door on the right."

My brother says, "Thank you." I doubt they hear him, because the door slams behind us.

My hungry eyes take in everything around me. I doubt I've been on this end of the complex before, even though I lived in this building for 14 years. It's very similar to the plain gray walls outside the glass dorm, except there are more signs on the doors. The one we are told to enter says, 'Office of the Complex Chief.' Across the hall, the door says 'Complex Employment Office.'

The pretty blonde assistant I remember following the complex chief into the glass dorm before my escape smiles at us from behind a desk. "May I help you?"

My brother smiles in his charming way. "Yes. We are here to see Mr. Athill, the complex chief. I am Brock Hamble, and these are my aides and my bodyguard."

"He is expecting you in the conference room. Please follow me."

We follow the bouncy blonde into a long, narrow room with an equally long, thin table in the center of it. The thin dark face of the complex chief watches us from the head of the table without expression. "Well, well, well. If it isn't the famous Brock Hamble."

Brock walks all the way to the head of the ever-long table and shakes the complex chief's hand. The man I grew up despising doesn't smile; he doesn't even move more than his arm during the greeting. Brock acts like he just received a warm welcome from a friend and sits down on the left-hand side of the table. The rest of us just sit down without attempting to shake the somber man's hand. I sit as far away from him as I can. He intimidates me, and I don't want him to see my fake wrinkles.

His yellow teeth stand out as he says, "You know, of course, why I arranged this meeting."

Brock grins and shakes his head. "No, I'm afraid I don't."

Mr. Athill glares at my brother. "You lied in this little pamphlet." The complex chief pulls the pamphlet I gave him at the mall out of his pocket and slaps it on the table. "A girl with short blonde hair gave this to me at your campaign booth in the mall."

Brock fakes a look of concern on his face. "Oh dear, you voted for me because you thought I was neutral to the Complex Law."

Spit flies out of Mr. Athill's mouth. "No, I did not vote for you!"

Brock patiently wipes a fleck of spit off his cheek and folds his hands in front of himself. "If you are not a disgruntled supporter, then why am I here?"

"Did your sister, Elira Hamble, give me this pamphlet?"

The man stabs his finger so forcefully into the pamphlet on the table, I'm afraid his thick, yellow fingernail might have gouged the table beneath it.

Brock picks a piece of lint off his sleeve as he says, "Why does it matter which of my volunteers gave it to you?"

"If I let her within arm's reach of me and didn't haul her back here where she belongs, I will never forgive myself."

Brock's eyes grow serious. "Let's cut to the chase. I assume that you are not happy that I plan to disband the Complex Law."

Mr. Athill chuckles to himself. "You are a dreamer, Mr. Hamble. The people of our country cannot support the lesser-functioning inhabitants of this building. I have at my disposal millions of dollars flowing through these walls to keep these deformed people alive and strong enough to work. Do your voters have millions of dollars to feed, clothe and house them?"

Brock raises his eyebrows. "Families will take care of their own."

"Not every person in this complex is as high functioning as your sister, nor has living family who will claim them."

"Then you can offer them a job here."

I clear my throat loudly. "Mr. Hamble, sir…"

"Eloise, let me finish. Under my proposed plan, those of adult age who are not claimed by their families will be given the option to leave on their own or to stay here to work for pay. All behavior drugs and hormone inhibitors will be removed from this building, of course."

"So you recognize that half of the streamlined manufacturing in this country happens in the city complexes."

"Yes, I do. The labs and machinery in this building won't go to waste, but people will be paid to work here, if they can stomach the place."

The complex chief leans toward my brother. "Unwanted little children can't work. What will happen to them?"

Brock doesn't bat an eye. "They won't stay here with you, they will be placed for adoption."

The grouchy, black-haired man throws his hands in the air. "No one will want them."

Brock smiles. "You underestimate humanity."

"I doubt it. I also doubt that you can get a majority to vote for this ridiculous plan of yours."

Brock shrugs. "I only need 51%. I got it once; I think I can get it again."

Rage fills the complex chief's eyes. "Do you know how many people you will put out of work if this happens? I employ over 200 people in this complex alone, and Herrington's complex row employs over 100 more."

Brock leans forward seriously. "Very true. Remind me again how many people work here for free?"

The man grows silent and scowls at my brother. "My employees won't vote for your anarchy and neither will any complex employee anywhere else. This is an uphill battle that you can't win. Just give up now."

Brock shakes his head. "Uh, no. I fully intend to shut you down within the year."

"Ahh, your little boy." The complex chief drums his fingers on the table for a minute. "Could your staff leave for a few minutes, so I can speak to you privately?"

My brother doesn't even flinch. "No, anything you want to say to me has to be said to all of us."

The complex chief leans forward. "I want what I'm about to say to be off the record." He looks pointedly at Damon, who has been taking careful notes throughout the meeting.

Brock smiles almost imperceptibly at the complex chief. He turns to Damon. "Put your pen down, Damon. This is not to be recorded. Do you give me your word, young man?"

Damon looks at the handle of Brock's briefcase and nods. "Yes, Mr. Hamble. You have my word."

Mr. Athill folds his hands in front of himself and lowers his voice. "Listen, Mr. Hamble. I could possibly pull some strings for your little boy. In fact, I will guarantee that your little boy will be able to stay in your home hidden from the world— if you leave the Complex Law alone."

Brock raises his eyebrows and shoots a quick look at me. "Huh, that is an interesting offer. I could keep my son prisoner in my own house and continue to worry that my escapee sister will be recaptured and brought back to this drug-controlled sweatshop, or I could repeal the Complex Law and both of the 'flawed' people I love, plus all the fine people who live here now could be free. Hmm. I choose to repeal the law." Brock stands up and gathers his things. "Thank you for inviting me to this enlightening meeting. Damon, did you get good notes on everything our fine friend said before the special favor was brought up?"

"Yes, I did."

"Excellent. I would shake your hand, Mr. Athill, but it doesn't look like you want to stand up, so we'll just show ourselves out. Thank you for your time."

The complex chief yells at our retreating backs, "It won't pass. Don't waste your breath, and if by some miracle it does pass, you will be personally responsible for the financial downfall of our country."

Brock turns around long enough to say, "Good day, Mr. Athill."

The door is almost shut when we hear, "I look forward to personally pinning a red button on your son when he arrives in a couple years, Mr. Hamble. You don't want me as an enemy."

"It's too late for that." Brock's hands are shaking when he forcefully shuts the door.

Chapter 24

WE MOVE SILENTLY from the conference room to the front door together. I look furtively around for anyone I might know down the long gray hall and I'm rewarded with a glimpse of Maxine carrying a box of something from the doctor's office, I'm guessing, to who knows where. I almost call out to her, but I stop myself.

Brock's bodyguard collects his weapons at the door and we stroll to our cars before speaking. I sidle up to my brother. "You were amazing in there, Brock. I was afraid you'd let him push you around like one of his employees, but you showed him who's boss."

My brother's frown turns into a smirk as he clicks off the camera on his briefcase. "He's worried. Could you tell? That is a very good sign for us."

Damon shakes his head. "I can't believe that last biting remark about your son. What a jerk."

Brock's jaw clenches. "I know. He's going to regret that." He then turns to his assistant. "Thank you, Jiang. I'm sorry I didn't let you get a word in edgewise. I'll see you tomorrow." Jiang bows respectfully to my brother. "Yes, Mr. Hamble, sir. I will see you tomorrow." My brother turns to the rest of us. "Damon, make sure you send me a copy of your notes."

"I will."

"Hop in, and I'll get you two home." We climb in and I become an Elira sandwich again, much to Damon's delight. I try to scoot my legs away from my admirer. I really miss Garth.

I look at my brother curiously. "Where are you staying tonight, Brock?"

"I think I'll stay at Mom and Dad's, and then I'll take the monorail in the morning. I'm too tired to travel more tonight."

"Will Chantilly be okay with you doing that?"

My brother's eyes dart around nervously. "Um, she decided to move in with her parents for a little while, so she doesn't even know where I am right now, unless she's watching the news, I guess."

I reach for his arm. "I'm so sorry. What happened?"

My brother keeps his eyes low. "She told me that if I tried

212

to repeal the Complex Law, she'd leave me. She wasn't kidding. She left two days ago with Joy."

That woman doesn't deserve my brother. I feel so bad for him. "I'm sure she'll have a change of heart once the baby is born. She'll love him so much, she'll want you to ensure his freedom."

"I hope so." *Ring, ring.*

Brock's burly bodyguard turns around. "Mr. Hamble, sir, do you want me to answer your car phone?"

"Yes, please."

The bodyguard's voice is deep and smooth. "Hello? Oh, yes. He's right here."

The bodyguard seems almost speechless for a moment. "Mr. Hamble, sir, it's the President of The United Cities on the line for you."

Brock raises his eyebrows. "Really? Put him on speaker phone." He quickly clicks the camera back on and takes a deep breath. "Hello? This is Senator Brock Hamble."

There is a long pause before we hear the President's deep voice. "Hello, Mr. Hamble. I feel like I know you so well, even though this is my first time speaking with you since I swore you in."

My brother chuckles. "Yes, I could say the same thing about you. Your changes to the Complex Law are legendary."

"So, you're letting me know that you don't like me, from the start."

Brock nods. "Basically."

"Well, to be honest, I don't like you either."

I love the smile on my brother's face. "Why not? Most people do these days."

"Cheeky. I don't like you because you are trying to undo 40 years of hard work—my life's legacy, you could say."

Brock looks at all of us with a self-assured smile before he answers. "I would say the timing of my actions is perfect for you. You are turning 80 in a year, are you not? I doubt you are looking forward to the accommodations at the Adanlay Complex for the Elderly."

The President's deep voice says slowly, "I am not as decrepit as you think I am, Mr. Hamble."

"I don't think you're decrepit at all. In fact, when I repeal the Complex Law, you won't have to go to the Complex for the Elderly."

"I have no intention of going into the Complex for the Elderly no matter what happens, young man."

"But our laws apply to everyone in the country, don't they? Even you?"

The President sniffs. "When you have spent 40 years of your life in public service, you will agree that you deserve a few perks for your efforts."

"So, you believe the law applies to everyone but you."

There is a lengthy pause. "Mr. Hamble, if you switched

sides on this thing, I'm sure I could make an exception for your immediate family as well."

"Well, that is something for me to consider, but do you think that it is fair to the rest of the country if they have to follow the laws that we wrote, but we don't?"

The President raises his voice. "Life isn't fair, Mr. Hamble. I have worked hard all my life to make this country one that we can be proud of. You don't want to undo all of that, do you?"

Brock shakes his head in disgust. "The thing that is different about your pride in our country and my pride in our country is that I think everyone has the right to make their own life what they want it to be; you think that only people who look and function like you do."

There is an audible sigh on the other end of the line. "I have been thinking about the comforts, or lack of them, in the complexes lately. I understand why you're doing this, Hamble. I don't agree with it, but I understand it."

Brock raises his eyebrows at me. "So where do we go from here?"

"I want the protests to stop. I want to be able to leave my house in peace again."

Brock leans toward the camera. "I want that too."

"If this joke of an idea doesn't pass, will you convince the people to stop accosting me?"

Brock pauses. "Yes, if you let us vote on it, I will convince my supporters to leave you alone, no matter how the vote turns out."

"You'll have to get one million signatures in order to get an emergency vote for this despicable thing. At least 51% of the people will have to vote for it to pass. If it does, you have a lot of social restructuring to do in every city so that the infrastructure of the country doesn't collapse."

"I have a plan in the works for a new infrastructure too. I want the best for this country, Mr. President. I will take care of everything."

"I'm sure you believe that, but if you have forgotten anyone or anything, the citizens of this country will be furious at you. You will go down in history as the man who took a peaceful country and dropped it on its head to bleed out until it ceased to exist."

Brock raises his eyebrows yet again. "Mr. President, I plan to go down in history as someone who did something brave, new, and ethically-correct for all citizens."

Chapter 25

I WAKE UP TO SOMEONE banging on our hideout door. Why did we tell so many people where they can find us? I slide out of bed and open the door. Damon is standing there smirking at me. "Good morning, sunshine. Okay, so we need one million signatures in order to get an emergency vote. Are you ready to divide and conquer?"

I wipe my eyes unenthusiastically. "Sure. That's what I do these days."

His smile droops. "Are you getting tired of this?"

I look around the room as I figure out a response. "Uh, I want the law to change, but—I want to go home. I miss Garth."

Damon's bright eyes lose their sparkle. "I—I thought maybe you liked this time away from him. We've been working so well together."

I hate hurting my friend, but he agreed to be friends, didn't he? "Damon, I like you. You are an amazing friend and a political genius, but I miss Garth. I—love him."

Damon rolls his eyes. "Okay. I can see you are burning out. I was going to give you and Greggory all of Herrington, but I've changed my mind. Could you pass out flyers on this side of town at least?"

He is such a go-getter. I should help him. He's helping Brock, and me. "Yeah. I—we can do that." I look at my brother who nods unenthusiastically from the couch.

Damon shifts his weight from foot to foot. "Do you at least want to meet me at the protestor's rally tonight?"

I really don't want to. Doesn't he ever take a break from politics? It gets exhausting after a while. "No. I—have something else I need to get done. I'm sorry, but maybe another time."

Damon takes a deep breath in and lets it out. "All right. Here's the flyers. Take care of yourself." Damon frowns as he squeezes my hand and walks out the door.

Greggory is looking at me with raised eyebrows from the couch. I slump next to him and scowl. He turns my grouchy face towards him. "I wondered if you were going to forget about Garth and fall for that guy."

I throw my hands in the air. "No. He's a great guy, but he's all work and practically no play. He is exhausting me."

"I don't know why he wants us to go door to door again. If they broadcast where people can sign the petition on the news, I bet half the city would flock there on their own."

I scowl at him. "Why didn't you tell him that?"

Greggory grins. "I liked watching you two make each other miserable too much."

I punch my brother in the arm. "That's not—nice."

He laughs. "I'm sorry. You deserve better." He kisses my forehead.

The wet spot on my forehead makes me realize how much my brother has done for me lately. I smile at him. "I know I haven't said it like I should, but thank you for helping me through all the craziness since we put the video on the news, Greggory."

He smiles at me and punches me back in the shoulder. "I finally realize after spending this time with you how much we missed out on while you were in the complex." He points to the picture of our family that we took with us from the news station. "You deserve to be happy. I see how much you miss Garth. He brings out the best in you."

The thought makes me a little bit teary. "Yes, he does." I nudge my brother with my elbow. "Does anyone make you happy?"

His eyes dart away from me. "Well, I do have someone on

my mind a lot. I'm the Damon in that story though. She's taken and she's not going to change her mind for a black sheep like me."

I hope he's ready to talk about this. "Avra?"

Greggory flips his face around to face me. "How did you know?"

I smile as I remember what my brother was like the first time I met him. "You became a kinder, gentler person after you met her. I've seen the affection you have for her in your eyes."

My brother frowns. "Well, it's a wasted effort. I need to be happy for her and Scott."

I pat my brother's knee in sympathy. "Yeah, probably. Avra and Scott are great together. Answer me this, what do you see in her? From what I gather of your former life," I gesture with my arm around the room, "it doesn't seem like she would be your type."

He smiles. "True. I don't know. I guess I like that she has so many problems and still manages to be happy and beautiful and kind. Not all girls are that way."

I smile at my rough-around-the-edges brother, because his character is shining through. "I get it." I look at the picture of our family again, and remember his promise to give it to me if I did something for him. "Hey—if I put in a good word for you with Avra, will you give me that picture?"

Greggory smiles to himself. "Yes. I will accept that deal."

I laugh to myself. "I promised Scott that I'd tell you to stay away from her."

He raises his eyebrows. "So does this mean that you're on my side?"

"More or less." I grin at my brother. "Why don't you call Damon and tell him your idea about advertising on the news."

He stands up. "Okay, why not." Greggory calls Damon on our ancient phone and explains his idea. "Perfect. We'll just wait on the flyers till after noon then. Good luck."

I just had a thought. "Does the government have any pull on what goes on the news and what doesn't?"

Greggory snorts. "Yeah, they do. In fact, Damon thinks he can sneak onto the news by sending protestors with the information on where to sign the petition on their giant signs. The news reporters love to show the annoying blockades that protestors and their signs cause on the news even if they've been told not to encourage the Complex Law repeal."

I nod my head. "That might just work."

My brother yawns and stretches his arms. "We're supposed to hold off on taking flyers until we've heard from him at noon."

I might have a free day… "Good. I—I want to break into Mom and Dad's house—to see Garth."

"Elira, that is a bad idea."

I feel my hopes evaporate. "I know, but I don't know if I can handle being away from him one more minute."

"There is a peace officer in the house at all times."

I look around the room for something that will help me. "What if I dressed up like a carpet cleaner or something? There has to be a way to get in there."

Greggory nods at my ingenuity. "We don't have a carpet cleaning machine though."

"Well, there must be something I can be."

He shakes his head like thinking hurts too much. "I can't think of anything that would make sense to fix in the basement."

I bat my eyelashes at him. "You could come with me and see Avra..."

My brother struggles within himself whether to be reckless or responsible. "I—I want to, but we are undesirables number one and number two right now."

I think of a compromise. "How about this—if Damon gets the news to broadcast where to sign the petition, we celebrate by breaking in to see our friends. If he doesn't, we spend the rest of the day going door to door with flyers—again."

Greggory shrugs. "Okay, I can live with that."

I shriek with delight. "Turn on the news. I want to know the minute your plan works." I get the paper and a pen out of the roll top desk to write Garth another note. *Knock, knock.* Who in the world can that be?

My brother leans against the door. "Who is it?"

"It's Jack Long. You are trespassing on my property."

I run behind the wall of boxes and signal with my hand that Greggory is going to have to deal with his friend. Greggory opens the door. "Jack, my friend! It's so great to see you after all these years! You've put on a pound or two."

Jack doesn't sound as enthusiastic. "You are such a punk, G. You could've at least asked for permission to use this place."

I can almost hear the smile I'm sure is on Greggory's face. "Sorry, man. We were in a bad situation and this was the only hiding place I could think of."

"That's funny, because when I was watching the news yesterday, the peace officers were completely bewildered how you could be hiding so well in this city. I knew immediately where you were. I came to see if I was right, and it looks like I am."

"Ha, ha. You were always a clever guy. Is this going to be a problem? We've cleaned up the place; it was an abandoned mess when we got here."

"Who's we?"

"Uh, my girlfriend and me."

"Nice try. Your escapee sister is here too, isn't she?"

Greggory sounds nervous to me. "No, man. I had a girl here for some fun the other day, but she's gone now. Do your parents know I'm here?"

"I'm sure my parents don't know and wouldn't care either. I—on the other hand might need a little somethin'-somethin' to keep my mouth shut..."

My brother's voice hardens. "Really, Jack? I thought we were friends, man."

"We are. I could turn you in for $20,000, but because we're friends, I won't do that. The thing is, my parents have kicked me out of their basement, and I'm a little short on cash. You're a little short on a hiding place, so I think we can help each other out. What do you say?"

"I don't have much, Jack. I'm away from my parents."

Jack's voice is insistent. "Open your wallet and let's see what's inside." I peer around the wall of boxes to see what my brother will do.

Greggory opens his wallet and pulls out the $150 that we have left to our names. "If I give this to you, I'm going to starve down here."

"That's not my problem. This will keep my lips sealed for two days. I'll be back in a couple days for your next installment of—rent."

Greggory raises his voice. "If I'm paying rent, then I demand some improvements in this hole."

"Not a chance, this is the best you're going to get. Have a nice day."

Chapter 26

AS SOON AS THE DOOR CLICKS, I walk out from behind the wall of boxes. "Well, I think my idea to go to Mom and Dad's house is getting better and better all the time."

My brother won't look at me and keeps shaking his head. "Jack is such a selfish jerk. I can't believe he would do that to me."

I smirk as I remember the first time I met Greggory. "I believe you wanted to know how much I was worth the first time you meet me."

My brother is silent for a minute. "I—yeah. He and I were

one and the same for years. Please tell me I'm less disgusting than him now."

I pat him on the back. "You are night and day different."

"Good. I'm going to estimate how much food we have left." He walks to the refrigerator. "We have about four meals in here, and Jack will be back for more money in two days..."

Ring, ring. Greggory shakes his head to clear it before he answers the phone. "Hello? Perfect. We won't worry about it then. Thanks, Damon. Bye."

A smile erupts on my face. "Damon got his petition information on the news, didn't he?"

"Uh, yeah, he did."

"So we are going home!"

"I guess so. I wonder if I can get some cash somehow too…"

"ARE YOU SURE this is how computer technicians dress?"

"Yeah, computer geeks can wear whatever they want, pajamas even. People are so desperate to have their computers fixed that they don't care what the person who does it wears."

I fidget with my plain red T-shirt and tan pants. "All right. I won't worry about these clothes then. Where are my sunglasses?"

"On the table, but I think real glasses would be better for Mom and Dad's basement."

Where could I get real glasses? "Maybe Laura Beckman will lend me some stuff again."

Greggory looks in our almost empty fridge again. "I bet she will. Let's go."

My friend has everything I need again, even some plastic name badges that don't specify a company. I'm going to be Laura Beckman and Greggory is going to be Pat Green. Apparently, Laura and her mother used to sell homemade fudge at the city fair and these are their nametags. I'm so happy they put "Pat" instead of "Patricia" on her mother's. Greggory wouldn't appreciate having to dress up like a girl.

We use Laura's telephone to call my parents' house. Greggory holds the phone out so I can listen in too, but he is our voice. "Hello, Mrs. Hamble. This is Pat Green from Computer Cronies Repair. We received a call from you a week ago about the computer in your basement having some problems. We would like to stop by within the hour to get that fixed for you. Will that work?"

There is a noticeable pause as my mother makes sense of who and what is happening. "Oh—I'm so glad you finally found time for us. I miss using that computer; it will be nice to have it fixed. How much will it cost me?"

"I'm guessing it'll be about $300 dollars. Is that going to be a problem, ma'am?"

"No, that will be fine. I'll have it ready for you."

"Thank you very much, Mrs. Hamble. My partner and I will see you in about 20 minutes."

"I look forward to it. Thank you."

We park around the corner to my parents' house, because we don't want the peace officer on the road staring at Greggory's car while we're inside. My heart flutters with excitement and bleeds at the same time. We have agreed not to stay longer than two hours. I calm my beating heart as we walk down the sidewalk.

Knock, knock. My mother's smiling face and the unsmiling face of the peace officer who flirted with me a week ago greet us at the door. My mother's voice is unnaturally happy. "Hello, Pat! I'm so excited that Computer Cronies sent you here today. I can't wait to have my basement computer working again." Oh, Mom. I wish I could hug you right now.

The peace officer looks at the two of us for a long time. Does he recognize me? Maybe we should have dressed Greggory like a woman... "So, how long will you two need to fix the computer?"

Greggory says as seriously as he can, "As long as it takes, officer."

The man in uniform raises his voice. "This house is under government scrutiny until further notice. I have been told not to let anyone linger here for longer than an hour. So, an hour is all you're going to get. Good luck and get to work."

Mother looks from us to the officer to us again. "I—uh, I'm so sorry to be making your job harder. I'll just show you to the computer. This way, please."

The peace officer follows us down the stairs, much to my annoyance. I ask my mother in an inconspicuous way, "What was that heavenly smell?"

Mother turns her head toward me, so the officer can't see her face. She rolls her eyes. "Oh, my cook was making strawberry cheesecake today. It must be done."

I see the peace officer lick his lips, but he does not change directions.

Mother presents the computer to us with extra flourish. "Here is the computer that isn't working. It sometimes won't turn on, other times it will turn on, but I can't access my favorite programs."

Greggory looks at Mother authoritatively. "I have seen this happen twice in the past week. We will get right on it."

Mother smiles and asks in her sweet way, "Do you need anything? Extension cords? A flashlight? A drink of water?"

The peace officer rolls his eyes and sits down on the sofa. I wish I was sitting on that sofa—with Garth. I clear my throat and disguise my voice so it's lower. "I would like a drink of water, if it isn't too much trouble, ma'am."

"Of course, it isn't too much trouble. I'll even bring you a slice of that wonderful-smelling cheesecake if you'd like."

"You're too kind, ma'am."

As mother leaves, she asks the peace officer, "Would you like a slice of cheesecake? I could use another pair of hands."

"Sure, thing, ma'am." The officer gets up and follows my mother up the stairs.

I know I should be more cautious, but I can't wait another minute. I rush to the bookshelf and pull the red book out. *Click.*

The face I've been dreaming about is suddenly right in front of me. "Elira!" Garth whispers excitedly as he wraps me in his arms. I want to laugh and cry at the same time, but I don't get to do either. Greggory shoves me into the hidden room and shuts the door.

My lips find his like they're traveling a one-way road that can never be forgotten. I break away from him long enough to say, "I only have a few minutes, but I just had to see you. I miss you so much." He kind of stinks, since he can't shower in here, but I've missed him so much that his stink is like perfume to me.

"I wish you didn't have to leave. Just stay with me." My boyfriend's longing tears at my heartstrings.

I shake my head. "The peace officer let two people in. He has to let two people out."

"Elira?" Avra's voice asks from the sofa.

I smile and drag Garth to the sofa with me. "Yes, Avra, it's me. Are you all right? I hear you can walk again."

She lights up like I've brought Christmas into their world

of darkness. "I can walk. I'm almost back to normal. Right, Scott?" Her boyfriend nods and smiles at me from beside her.

I squeeze her hand. "I'm so glad."

Garth pulls me back up, kisses me, and then holds me against his shoulder. "Are you safe? What's going on out there?"

How much should I say? "We're trying to get a million signatures, so we can have an emergency vote about the Complex Law."

His posture straightens. "How many do you have so far?"

"I don't know. I have been trying to stay away from Damon today." Oops. I shouldn't have let that slip out.

Garth's eyes narrow. "Why?"

"He admitted today that he's still interested in me—but I'm not interested in him! I just want to be with you, Garth. I miss you so much."

The door swings open. My brother calls in, "I can hear them lingering at the top of the stairs. You better get out now."

I take the two notes out of my pocket and hand them to my boyfriend. Greggory waves to Avra and starts pulling me out the door. I kiss Garth one more time and hold his hand as long as I can. "I love you, Garth. Don't forget me."

"I won't. You're all I think about in here. Stay safe."

Click. I feel like my heart has been ripped out of my chest. That was not nearly long enough. I slump into a computer chair and pretend to be interested in the screen as I hear my mother's loud voice approaching. She is holding two plates of cheesecake and so is the peace officer. She exclaims, "Look at that! You got it to turn on. Why don't you take a little break and have some cheesecake?"

I glare at the peace officer like he is responsible for the hole in my heart. "Thank you, ma'am, but if we only have an hour, we better get this finished first."

The officer can't take his eyes off the plates he's holding. "Oh, I'll just subtract the time it takes you to eat from your total time here. Let's dig in."

Greggory snatches one of the officer's plates. "Okay, if you say so."

We sit in an awkward silence at the downstairs table as we eat our cheesecake. The peace officer's eyes never leave our faces. I think we better just wrap this up and get out of here.

I gulp down my last bite and give my brother a loaded look. "Come on, Pat. Back to work we go."

Greggory looks sideways at the peace officer's intense gaze. "Okay, Laura."

We pretend to fiddle around with the cords and click on as many menus as we can, so the man in uniform can't tell that we aren't doing anything. Greggory raises his eyebrows at me and I nod. It's time to be done. He clears his throat. "Mrs. Hamble, your computer is as good as new. That will be $300."

My mother hands me a wad of cash before the peace officer says, "Just wait a minute here. $300 for an hour of work?

I don't think even the good doctor who owns this house gets paid that much."

"When you hire the best, you have to pay for it," Greggory says without batting an eyelash.

"What is the name of your boss? I'd like to have a word with him about his prices."

"His name is—uh, Mr. Comp."

The peace officer narrows his eyes. "Mr. *Comp* owns the *comp*uter repair company you work for. What is his phone number?"

Greggory shrugs. "Oh, he just got a new one, so I'm not sure what it is."

"Okay, well, where is your office located? I'll just drop by."

Greggory is running out of ideas. "It's—uh, actually, just…"

"That's it." The peace officer jumps on Greggory and pushes him to the ground.

My brother yells, "Run! Don't look back. Run!"

I don't need telling twice. I bolt to the outside door and race through it. I can hear my heart and my breathing as loud as anything as I run around the corner and jump into Greggory's car. I forget my driving anxiety and step on the gas. The sleepy peace officer camped out on my parents' road looks at me quizzically for a few seconds and then pulls onto the road to follow me. I don't know what to do. I have to lose this guy. I speed up and take a right, then a left, then zip around a bunch of buildings I recognize vaguely. I think I'm getting near the car wash, actually. I don't see the peace officer behind me as I approach my hideout. Should I drive around longer? I'm afraid I'll get lost. I'm going in. Once I'm through the plastic strips, I shut off the car and run down the stairs to my room.

Tears are streaming down my face as I shut the door behind me. "Elira, what's wrong?" a deep voice asks from behind me.

Chapter 27

"DAMON, WHAT ARE YOU DOING HERE?" I ask through my tears.

"I came to tell you that we got to a million votes nationwide half an hour ago. Why are you crying?" he asks as he wraps me in his arms.

I collapse on his shoulder. "Greggory is gone. Peace officers took him. I had to run for it so they didn't take me too. What have I done?"

He pats my back gently. "Where were you?"

"My parents' house."

Damon frowns at me. "That house is under surveillance. Why on earth did you go there?"

"Well, the man who owns this car wash found us and demanded money to keep quiet, so we needed to get some money from my parents. We posed as computer repair workers."

"Elira! I would have given you the money you needed or found you a new place to stay. That was an unnecessary risk."

I don't look in his eyes. "I know. I just really wanted to see Garth again."

Damon's arms drop from around me. "Oh. That's really why you did it."

I pull the wad of cash out of my pocket. "I still got the money I need to stay here four more days."

He scoffs. "That's a terrible price to pay for this dump."

I wipe my eyes with a finger. "I know. I just don't know what else to do."

Damon's eyes soften. "Well, four days may be all you need. Since we got the required signatures, Brock called the President and insisted that we vote whether to repeal the Complex Law or not in five days."

I raise my eyebrows. "That's so soon. How will Alexander Prystine ever agree to that?"

Damon snickers. "Well, it sounds like angry mobs have been surrounding the President's house for a few days and he can't take it anymore. He agreed to have the vote on Thursday."

I collapse onto the couch. "I can't believe it. This could work." The reality of where my brother is suddenly comes back to me full force. "I—I just hope they don't hurt Greggory and my friends in the complex too much before then."

Damon joins me on the couch. "I don't think they'll hurt him, but they will definitely keep him locked up until after the emergency vote."

A sigh escapes my lips. "I can last five days. If the repeal doesn't pass, I'll just have to figure something else out—I've never been completely alone before."

Damon looks around the storage room I'm now calling home. "I would be happy to stay here with you. Or—you could even stay at my place." His hand finds my knee.

I scoot away. "No! That is not going to happen, Damon."

"I just want to help you. I won't touch you—unless you ask me too."

I shiver. "I'll be fine sleeping here alone." I turn my back on him as I calm myself down.

"Elira, don't be mad at me. Is there anything you'll let me do for you?"

I turn back around to face him, hating myself for what I'm about to ask. "Is there any way you could buy me some dinner?"

I HAVE NEVER BEEN THIS ALONE before.

Damon insists that he is bringing me dinner every day until the emergency vote. Yesterday he took me to his apartment building and showed me how to grill steaks. He was a little bit annoyed when I wanted to wander around his apartment complex looking for Maxine. I didn't find her. Today he brought me a giant meatball sandwich and a bag of chips after he got off work. He wants me to witness the vote tally on Thursday. I agree to go with him and I'm thankful for a way to make my meager food stretch. When I take my disguise back to Laura, I apologize that Greggory's disguise is with him in solitary.

She hugs me the way my mother would. "That's just fine. I'm not worried about those things. What I am worried about is whether the country is going to vote to repeal the Complex Law or not."

I nod in agreement. "I know. I'm worried too. We've come so far, I'd hate to be defeated at the last moment."

Laura looks into my sad eyes. "I just made some cookies. Would you like to take a plate of them home?"

"Yes! I mean, uh, yes, please. That would be very nice." I am an embarrassment when I'm worried about starving to death.

Laura loads the plate of cookies awfully high for a single person. I wonder why until I get back to the hideout and discover a twenty-dollar bill beneath them. It brings tears to my eyes. I hope I can help her as much as she has helped me.

KNOCK, KNOCK. I hate waking up this way. I don't have Greggory to calm my anxiety. Jack, my brother's greedy friend is here to collect his "rent." I pull my hair over my eye and just pay it, thankful that he isn't turning me in for the bounty on my head.

At lunchtime, I eat my last apple and the last five crackers from the bottom of the last box. My food is officially gone. My stomach growls with discomfort. Will I be able to last until Damon comes with spaghetti tonight? I'm feeling awfully hungry and alone when the phone rings. It's my mother! It is such a weird conversation.

"Hello?"

"Hello, this is Florence Hamble. I would like to order a large wooden bench."

"Mom! Oh, Mom, I miss you. I want to come home."

Her voice cracks a little. "I—I want the cushion to be soft and comfortable."

"Mom, I have enough money and food to last until the vote day, but that's all I have. I don't know what I'll do if the repeal doesn't pass."

"I don't care if it costs more, I only want things that I love in my yard."

"Mom, if there is any way to come see me, will you do it?"

239

"Yes, that will work. Thank you very much. I will pick it up tomorrow or the next day."

"Goodbye, Mom. I love you."

"Goodbye and have a nice day."

I wish.

I get so tired of sitting around by myself in my dark basement room that I take Greggory's car out and drive around the city for a while. I don't go very far away because I'm afraid I'll get lost or that someone will recognize this car. I drive by my parents' house to see if the peace officer is still parked outside. He is. I eventually end up in the parking lot of a grocery store. I use the $20 Laura gave me to buy enough food to get me through Thursday, the emergency vote day.

I stand next to an old man in the line to check out. He looks familiar to me. I must be lonely, because I say to him, "Excuse me. Are you Elmer?"

He looks confused. "I am Elmer. I'm sorry, but I don't know who you are."

"I am one of the troubled youth that Dr. Hamble taught to drive on your property."

The man looks at me knowingly. "Oh. I know who you are." He lowers his voice. "Everyone I know will be at the city building Thursday morning voting to repeal the Complex Law."

I step back, surprised. "Why do you think I care about that?"

Elmer whispers in my ear. "You are his daughter, Elira."

I look away. "I don't know why you would think that."

"I may be old, but I'm not stupid."

His eyes bore into mine as I ask, "Do you really think the repeal will pass?"

He lowers his voice. "Yes, I do. Everyone 70 and up will vote to repeal it, everyone who has had a child taken away to a complex will vote to repeal it, and anyone who saw that video of the complex on the news will vote to repeal it. I say your chances of being a free woman soon are very good."

I feel tears forming in my eyes. "Thank you, Elmer. I needed this encouragement today."

Chapter 28

I PRETEND THAT MY MUFFIN TASTES GOOD as I shove it into my mouth. This morning the national news station has been broadcasting only stories about people who like the Complex Law and want to keep it. It leaves me feeling like we have no chance of repealing it tomorrow.

Knock, knock. You have got to be kidding me. I paid Jack yesterday. He shouldn't come again until tomorrow. I am ready to give him a piece of my mind when I open the door to find Ernestine standing there.

"Ernestine!" I wrap my arms around her and refuse to let go even when she tries to pry me off. "How are you doing, kid?"

A sob escapes my lips. "I've never been alone like this. I hate it. Today the news is showing a lot of people who want the Complex Law to stay the same, and if it does, I am going to hate my life."

"One news story doesn't mean nothing. Keep your chin up."

My eyes scan her face for a reaction. "How is everyone?"

She grins. "I have another note for you." She lets me take it immediately this time. I unfold it and read it as I lovingly hold and sniff the pages. "So, what does lover boy have to say?"

The corners of my mouth creep up. "That he misses me and loves me. Avra is almost completely back to normal... Actually, you know all of this. You stay with them."

"Actually, I don't. Rocky and I moved back in with Frank like you suggested."

I lean forward excitedly. "Really? How is that going?"

Ernestine looks surprisingly emotional. "I—I'm not going to lie. It was the best choice I've made in a long time. We are living like a family again, and—it's wonderful."

I bite my lip as my heart sings. "I'm so happy to hear that! Are peace officers stopping by to check for escapees?"

Ernestine nods and finishes my bottle of water that is sitting next to the couch. "They do about once a week. I have two hiding places ready to go in that house, so we've been fine."

I carefully and lovingly fold my note back up. "So how did you get this note?"

"I stopped by your dad's office to hear the latest news on their situation and he gave the note to me to give to you."

My nose crinkles. "You've been visiting my dad at his office? Why didn't I think of that?"

She shrugs at me. "I'm sure he would love to see you again."

I shove the note into my pocket. "As soon as you leave, I'm going straight there."

"I won't hold you up then. Just know that the house is still under constant surveillance and your parents are not allowed to go to Brock's banquet tomorrow unless they bring their personal peace officers."

"No!"

She sneers as she nods. "Yeah, they've decided not to go, so you'll be able to go without as many officers there watching your every move."

I look at the picture of our family next to the couch. "They do so much for me."

"They are amazing people. You should really go hug your dad, kid."

I DECIDE TO TAKE A BUCKET BATH and just leave my hair the way it is. I'm tired of wigs. My eye makeup, Sparkly Clean Car Wash hat, and sunglasses are all the disguise

I use as I get ready to see my dad. Greggory's car is getting low on gasoline. I hope I have enough to get through today, because I don't have any money left.

For some reason, my driving has improved a lot since Greggory was captured. I wonder if having no choice but to drive myself has anything to do with it. My eyes scan the streets carefully looking for the giant ice cream cone building. I breathe a sigh of relief when I see it. The sign on the corner says Medical Parkway. Perfect. I park Greggory's car as far away from the door to the building as possible.

A woman supports her husband's arm as they leave the building ahead of me. I open the door for them. They smile at me and thank me as we pass. I bet they will vote to repeal the Complex Law tomorrow. His heart is giving him problems, I think. The waiting area is full of people. I knew it would be like this, but my heart starts pounding in apprehension anyway. I wander to the woman behind a tall desk.

"Excuse me, I would like to see Doctor Hamble."

"Do you have an appointment?"

"No... But I need to see him as soon as I can."

The woman doesn't even look at me as she says, "Walk-ins have to wait until everyone else with an appointment is seen first. Fill out this form and take a seat."

I really don't have time for this. A small mirror on the wall reflects my car wash hat back at me. Ooh, I have an idea. "I am afraid that Dr. Hamble's car was damaged at our car wash and we would like to make it right with him."

The woman looks at me this time. "Oh, oh dear. That poor man has had the worst luck lately. I will bring him out to you as soon as I can. Have a seat."

I sit next to two motherly-looking women in the waiting room and can't help but overhear their conversation. "Yes, you'll absolutely love Dr. Hamble. I was so lucky that the problem with my aorta wasn't detected until I was age nine. I could've spent the last 30 years in the complex, but Dr. Hamble has taken amazing care of me and he doesn't let anyone else, especially the government, know about it."

"I think I've had my murmur for a long time, too. I can't believe they didn't send me to the complex. I am just sick of my other doctor though. He has the bedside manner of an ape. I'm voting to repeal the Complex Law tomorrow. Are you?"

"Yes. Absolutely."

The creak of a door opening makes my head jerk in that direction. My dad walks towards me in a white lab coat. His eyes light up, but he keeps the rest of his face neutral. "So I hear there has been an accident with my car. Should we go outside and look at it?"

"Yes. I'm so sorry, sir."

"It's okay, we'll figure it out."

As soon as we get to my dad's car, he motions for me to get

in. As soon as the door clicks, I gush, "Dad, I miss you so much. I want to come home."

His big warm hands envelop mine. "I know, honey. It must be really hard since they took Greggory away. Mom and I are struggling with that, too."

"Yes! It's terrible! It was all my fault too. I wanted to see Garth so bad."

Dad's tired face sighs. "I hate having a child taken away again, even if it's just for a while. Luckily, he's toughened up a lot this past year."

My eyes focus on him. "We've been living in a dirty hole, and he's been fine. His random skill set has been surprisingly helpful for us."

My father seems astonished. "Huh, that's good to know. I'm hoping that tomorrow will change everything. No more living apart; no more living in fear."

I bite my lip with worry. "What if people vote to keep the Complex Law?"

"I'll make sure you're taken care of, honey." He opens his wallet and pulls out all of the cash he has and gives it to me. It looks like it's around $80. "You won't have to stay in the car wash anymore. Just come here and make the same kind of excuse as you did today to see me."

I let out a long breath. "I just hope it works out tomorrow."

"Me too."

DAMON IS ALL SMILES as he picks me up to go out to dinner. "This is our last dinner together before the law changes, so I want it to be extra special."

I frown. "I don't have any fancy clothes."

"You look fine just how you are."

Damon's car is silver with stacks of boxes, books, buttons, and pamphlets in the back seat. I raise my eyebrows. "You let your job take over your life, you know."

He shrugs. "I love my job, and I would give up my back seat for a less worthy cause than the one we're fighting for right now." He reaches over and squeezes my hand. "You're going to be a free woman soon, Elira."

I have a vision of the Complex Law not being repealed, and Garth having to stay in my parents' secret bunker forever. I might have to give up on Garth and give in to Damon, handing out pamphlets door to door for the rest of my life. I sniff as I imagine how probable that future is.

We arrive at an Italian restaurant and Damon takes my arm as we walk in. The host is not particularly friendly. "How many for you tonight?"

"Two, please."

"Right this way."

Damon smiles at me. "You will love their breadsticks."

"Is this table all right?"

Damon nods. "Yes. It's perfect, thank you."

I try to hide my dislike of being placed in the middle of the dining room. Garth knows that I would much rather be in the corner, away from everyone's eyes.

Damon looks at the menu only briefly. "I love pasta. I think I'll have the shrimp scampi. What are you in the mood for?"

I only look at the first part of the menu. "I don't really care. I guess I'll try the lasagna."

A big, burly man in an expensive suit approaches our table. "Are you Damon Bellvue?"

My friend seems excited to be recognized. "Yes, I am."

I don't like the sneer on the man's face. "You work for Brock Hamble, don't you?"

"Yes, I do."

The man's voice lowers considerably. "Well, I'd like you to take a look at the crowd of people in the corner there." We turn around to see thirty well-dressed people glaring back at us. "We are having a meeting about how to stop what you and Hamble are trying to do."

Damon won't be bullied. "You should feel lucky that you are the part of the population who have the right to meet together and try to change things."

The man pokes Damon in the chest. "We have rights, because we have the superior brain function for keeping this country strong and successful. You look like a strapping young man. Do you really want to risk mixing your fine genes with flawed ones?"

I don't like how long Damon pauses before answering the man. His eyes never leave mine. "I will let my heart, not my genetic superiority, decide who I mix genes with."

The man leans closer to us. "You have made a lot of people with excellent resources very angry. I would watch my back if I were you." He turns around and sits with his scowling friends again.

Those people give me the creeps. I lean forward. "Damon, what do we do now?"

His mouth doesn't smile as he watches his food get placed before him. "I don't care what they do to me. We continue our cause and let the people vote for what they want tomorrow."

I'm sure the lasagna is better tasting than my brain is telling me it is, but I've lost my appetite. The people in the corner keep raising their voices about how upset they are about people trying to ruin the country. I'm thankful when they finally leave the restaurant. Our waiter has not filled our glasses in quite a while. Damon says he is not going to get a good tip. When our waiter finally shows up, he brings our bill, but no drinks. He scowls at us as he says, "If you want to fill our tables with people who can't take care of themselves, then maybe you should eat somewhere else next time." He turns on his heel and walks to the next table.

What a jerk. Damon slaps some money on the table and

251

stands up. He leans toward the waiter's back as he says loudly, "No problem. I will be glad to take my business somewhere else. Come on, good-looking, let's go." Did he just call me good-looking?

I just want to get in the car and get out of here. Unfortunately, Damon's car won't be going anywhere. When we find his car in the parking lot, the windshield and the back windows have been bashed in and all four tires have been slashed. All of the Brock Hamble pamphlets, buttons, and flyers from the back seat are burning in a pile next to the car.

Damon just stands there staring at the fire and his car. I finally tug on his arm, uncomfortable with all of the eyes peeking at us from their own vehicles and the windows of the restaurant. "I'm so sorry, Damon, but we need to get out of here. How are we going to get home?"

My friend sighs. "I just hope the jerk inside will let us use the phone to call a cab."

Chapter 29

DESPITE THE SCARY MOB of people that destroyed Damon's car last night, I am so glad that we weren't hurt and today has finally come. Whether the people of the country vote to repeal the Complex Law or not, I will quit living in limbo. I may end up washing dishes at Toto's Pizzeria and bouncing from one friend's house to another until I can find a tiny place of my own, but it will be a relief to know where my future is headed. My optimism even allows me to force a smile when Jack stops by to collect his 'rent' again.

Brock calls me as I get dressed. "I want to take you to the complex tomorrow, to free your friends little sister."

I sigh in exasperation. "That will only happen if enough people vote for it. Do you know what happened to Damon and me last night? Don't count your ducks before they're hatched."

"You mean chickens."

"Oh, right. Sorry."

Brock laughs. "You are so funny. We should hang out more; I need someone who can make me laugh these days. In all seriousness though, I did hear about you and Damon. I've had the same thing happen to me a couple of times. I've had to hire an extra bodyguard to guard my vehicle everywhere I go."

I practically growl, "That is ridiculous. I hope today is the last day of anger and frustration about the law for the country."

My brother's voice perks up. "That's the spirit. Your job is to think positive. I will be in Adanlay for the vote, so Damon will look out for you at the Herrington Convention Center."

"I assumed it would be the two of us. Thanks, and good luck, Brock. Thanks for everything."

DAMON CALLS ME and offers to pick me up in his rental car, but I'm feeling a little bit wary after last night, and I want to drive myself. My gut tells me that I need to prepare myself to live alone from now on. I hope that no one will recognize me. Everyone in the city knows that Elira Hamble has been sneaking around in disguises helping her brother, Brock

Hamble. I feel like no disguise I choose will be good enough for the prying eyes and heated tempers of the people of Herrington. I guess the black wig Ernestine left here will do. I gather everything I want to keep from this place and stick it in a box. The pictures of our family and Greggory's blanket are the most valuable things in here. I throw my brother's plain clothes that we bought together and my own in as well, though. This box is going with me tonight.

Thankfully, my dad gave me enough cash yesterday to fill up Greggory's car. Damon is waiting for me at the door of the convention center when I arrive. This is the place we were at last week. He rushes out to me and takes my arm as we walk in. He whispers in my ear, "It's time to know how the world feels about basic human rights, Elira. The people standing in line with me at the voting booth today seemed—divided." Of course they were.

I get through security at the door without being recognized. I just plan to keep my face to the wall as much as possible. "Damon, I'm starving. Can we eat first?"

"Sure, let's get a plate." It feels like deja vu when Douglas Shriner welcomes us from the stage. He goes on and on about the virtues of voting for whatever Brock wants because he is such an amazing senator. I wonder if he even knows what we're voting on. This is about changing history—150 years of bigotry, to be exact. I look around the enormous room and sigh. This is exactly the same setting I was in a week ago. It's exactly the same food, exactly the same sponsors, exactly the same process of watching the big screen as the votes come in. The only thing that isn't the same is that the people I love aren't here… A tear leaks out of my eye as I think of Greggory in isolation, Brock leaving his empty house in Adanlay with only two bodyguards for support, my parents being held prisoner in their own house, Scott, Avra, and Garth peeing in a bucket in a hidden room with no windows. Has the cost of this moment been too great?

Douglas Shriner smiles at us and directs our attention to the big screen. "The first two cities have posted their voting results. It looks like the Complex Repeal has 40% of the vote so far. The other 60% wants to leave the Complex Law alone. Oh, and here is another city. The Complex Repeal is at 42%. The wonderful thing about tonight is that there is only one thing to count on the ballots. The results should come in much quicker than last week. Oh, here is another city. The Complex Repeal is at—uh, 41%."

Damon bumps me with his shoulder. "Hey, don't give up hope. If it doesn't pass, we'll try again next year."

I imagine dragging the last few days of my life out over a year. My head sinks to the table. I'm pretty sure my wig is askew, but I don't care. I can't keep living like this. Maybe I'll drive to the mountains and find one of the waterfalls my dad was talking about. I think living behind a waterfall will be ten times better than this. Applause erupts around me. I sit up and look at the screen. The Complex Repeal is at 44%. Woohoo. It's not going to pass. I suddenly feel sick. "Damon, where is the bathroom? I don't feel well."

Concern fills his eyes. "Out the door and to the left. Do you need help?"

"No! I mean, no thank you. I'll be fine." I wobble out into the hall. The ladies room isn't too far away. I am struggling to keep my dinner on the inside as I burst through the door. A woman is about to walk into a stall but I push her out of the way and barely get my barf to the porcelain bowl in time. I apologize with my eyes as I lock the stall and flush. I sit on the toilet fully clothed and bawl my eyes out.

When I finally leave my stall, I'm surprised to see the woman I pushed still standing there. She gently places a hand on my arm. "Have you been drinking, honey?"

I wipe my eyes with the back of my hand. "No. I just have a lot to lose if the Complex Law isn't repealed."

"You too, huh. You're in good company tonight. I was really hoping to see my daughter after 15 years tomorrow. It doesn't look like it's going to happen though, does it?"

"No," I say as tears start falling again. The kind woman wraps me in her arms and lets me bawl on her shoulder. When I finally pull away, she looks at me curiously and points to my left eye. I look in the mirror and see that my tears have washed away my cheap makeup out from under my eye. A purple streak is plain for all to see. I left my makeup in the car. How will I get to it without anyone recognizing me?

The woman takes some toilet paper and tries to help me fix my makeup. "You're Elira Hamble. I understand now why you're so upset about the voting."

My bottom lip trembles. "I'm tired of living in hiding." The woman nods at me and squeezes my hand.

Suddenly Damon bursts into the ladies room. "Elira! Get out here!"

The woman frowns at him. "Get out of here, young man; this is the ladies room!"

"But, the last votes just came in. It passed! The Complex Law has been repealed with 53% of the vote!"

Chapter 30

I'M FREE. I CAN'T BELIEVE IT. Tears stream down my face in torrents. So much for my makeup. I wish Garth or Avra or my Mom or one of my brothers was here to hug me. Damon hugs me, and though it's not the hug I want most, I'm thankful for his friendship. Something suddenly surges through my veins. I'm not sure if it's adrenaline, or rage, or what, but I am not waiting for Brock to take me to the complex tomorrow. In fact, I will not wait a moment longer. I'm going to free Shasta right now. I hug the kind woman and thank her before I rush out of the bathroom.

"Elira? Where are you going?" Damon asks as he follows me.

"I'm going to the complex."

He grabs my hand and pulls me to a stop before shaking his head at me. "I don't think that is a good idea. Wait for the dust to settle on this. Go tomorrow."

"No. I'm going now."

"The complex chief will keep doing what he's doing until he's ordered to do something else. It's 11:00 pm. He won't get his new orders until tomorrow."

"I. Don't. Care."

"Elira, he might lock you up for the night."

"I'd like to see him try."

I don't wait to hear what else Damon has to say. I march to Greggory's blue car and fly out of the parking lot as fast as I can. I probably should go get Garth first, but this fire in my veins won't let me. I want my friends out, and I want them out now.

When I arrive at the complex, I march to the front doors, and I'm angry to see that two guards are still there ready to cause me trouble. I don't have any patience for this. I yell at them, "The Complex Law is repealed. It's done. Let me in. I have people I want out of there."

A deep voice says, "I'm sorry ma'am, but we still have orders to remain at our posts for the safety of all residents and their families. If you have a legitimate claim to someone inside, you will have to fill out the paperwork necessary to reclaim them."

"Nope. I'm going in right now."

"I'm sorry, ma'am, but I can't let you…"

I push them out of the way and pull on the door knob. "These are citizens with the same rights as you have. If you try to stop me, I'll see you in court."

One of the guards lays his hands on me as one of the front doors opens. The complex chief peeks his head out. "Ah, I had a feeling I would be seeing you tonight, Elira Hamble."

I shake the guard's hand off of me. "I wish I had something kind to say, but I don't, Mr. Athill. I'm here for Shasta, and I will not leave without her."

He folds his arms in front of his chest. "She is not your flesh and blood. You cannot take her."

Anger rages in me. "She is not your flesh and blood either, so you cannot keep her. If you want to take this to court, I'm sure Shasta will say that she wants to be with me instead of you during this time of transition."

The yellow-teethed man glowers at me. "I have been given instructions in the last half an hour to only let people go if their families have the proper paperwork that links them. These instructions came from your delightful brother himself."

I lose my patience. "You are basically out of a job, Mr. Athill. Why are you standing here fighting with me? You should just go home and rethink your life. I have as many rights as you have, and I know what Shasta has been going through in here. She's leaving with me tonight." I push past him and enter the building. I feel the pressure of his hand on my shoulder. I brush it off roughly. "Don't you ever touch me again."

I don't know why, but he lets me walk past him. He just glares at me as I march down the gray halls. I'm hoping I'll figure out where Shasta is. When the doors stop having plaques, I start knocking. I know it's late and everyone is in bed, but someone is going to answer. The first door I knock on is a male dorm. I smile and apologize to the male mentor who peeks through the crack in the door. Well, I'll just move on to the next dorm. Mentor Briggs answers the door. I feel sweat forming on my forehead. What have I done? I am an idiot. This place is full of people who hate me. I should've waited to come here with my senator brother. No one would question him. I'm going to get smacked by the man who hauled Bicep to his death and broke my toes earlier this year.

"Sorry, Mentor Briggs, wrong door."

"Do I know you?"

I turn my head so my purple birthmark isn't easily visible. "I'm with the committee to reunite complex residents with their families now that the Complex Law has been repealed. I am trying to find the female glass dorm."

"I can't believe people voted to repeal the law. We've lived this way for 150 years. Whatever. At least my neighbors will quit harassing me for working here. The female sixteens and seventeens are one more door down."

"Thank you. Have a nice night." Mentor Briggs grunts and closes the door.

I feel my hand shaking as I raise my fist to the door of the glass dorm. I escaped from here not all that long ago. I knock hard and purposefully. When Mentor Roberta answers the door, I feel my knees start to buckle. If I can confront the complex chief, I can confront her.

"Mentor Roberta, I am here for a red-buttoned girl named Shasta."

She looks at her watch. "Why do you need her this late at night?"

I flip my hair out of my eye, so she'll know who she's dealing with. "Because the Complex Law has been repealed and she will be leaving with me."

Mentor Roberta's eyes grow huge. "Elira? Is that you?"

"Yes. My brother is the most influential senator in the country right now and I am so full of hatred for this place, I would highly suggest giving me Shasta before I do something drastic."

My former mentor's eyes narrow at me. "I can't believe they let you in here. The complex chief hates you more than anyone else in the world."

"I'm sure he does, but he doesn't have the power to keep

anyone here anymore. I require my friend, Shasta, this minute, or I will put another exposé on the news highlighting you."

"Fine! Get your friend. She will probably die soon anyway and get out of here."

Die soon? I push past Mentor Roberta and run to my old dorm room. The lights are off and I can hear girls snoring and sleeping deeply. I turn left and find Shasta's old bed—empty. What happened to her?

"Who are you? What are you doing here?" I recognize that voice.

"I've come for Shasta."

"She's by the window. She is really sick because she insists on sleeping in a place that lets toxins seep in." Ah, it's my former favorite roommate, Vanessa.

"Good. She's a smart girl. There are no toxins outside."

The redhead doesn't listen. "Yes there are. I won't go anywhere near that window."

"I don't have time for this. You'll find out tomorrow that you have been lied to your whole life. Embrace the window and the outside. I just came from out there and it is toxin free."

Vanessa shuts up, either out of exasperation or disbelief. I rush to Shasta's bed. She is sleeping like the dead. "Shasta, wake up!"

My tall, skinny friend moans, "I can't work so soon. I need more sleep. My hands..."

"Shasta, it's me, Elira. I have come back for you. Get up and I will take you away from here."

As I set Shasta upright she squints her eyes at me. "I don't feel so good. I think I remember you. You were the one who escaped and everything changed around here after that. Things got worse. Why did you do that?" Why doesn't she remember me?

"I'm sorry things got worse. Things are about to get better. I'm taking you away from here. I'm taking you to a safe place with Avra and my mom. The beds are soft and my dad will fix your hands. He's a doctor."

Shasta slowly stands up. "I need help walking any farther than the bathroom. Will you help me?"

Oh, no. Why is she so much worse than I left her? "Yes, Shasta. Let's go."

I help my friend put some shoes on and stand up. "I have a car, Shasta. I will drive you away from here."

"What is a car?" Wow, did I used to be like this?

"Don't worry. I will teach you everything you need to know."

As we shuffle through the door, Mentor Roberta stops us in the common room. "You were a fool to come here tonight, Elira. I'm not letting you leave."

"Yes, you are."

Roberta's face twists with rage. "You have made this job so difficult, young lady. I am hated by everyone who knows where I work. I even occasionally feel bad when I see these girls come back from work, crying without tears, but this is a job that has to be done, and I have done it well for 30 years. You are not going to waltz out of here again, ruining everything I've worked for."

I laugh humorlessly. "Oh yes I am. The votes are in; I have rights now. Shasta has rights now. She doesn't want to stay here, and you would be a fool to try and make her."

The door behind Mentor Roberta opens and the complex chief walks in. "Roberta, just let her go. This place is finished. Let's just leave it in shambles so they can appreciate the good we did."

The angry mentor shakes her head in disbelief. "I can't believe this place is finished. We've lived this way for 150 years; the people on the outside are not ready to face what we see on the inside."

I angrily wipe the rest of the makeup off my eye. "Let's find out if people can handle it, right here, right now."

She spits as she leans toward me. "You are a disgrace, Elira Hamble. I hope I never see you again."

I wipe my arms on the side of my shirt. "The feeling is mutual. Please unlock the door."

Mentor Roberta doesn't move; she just glares at me. The complex chief walks to the door and unlocks it. I haul Shasta out with me as fast as I can. I don't want him to change his mind. The complex chief starts walking. "If you'll just follow me, rebellion leader, I'll take you to the front door."

I stop in my tracks as I think about who else is here. "Actually—I would like to collect Jefrey Yesterly as well."

The complex chief turns around and looks at me curiously. "He turned in your late friend, Avra, for money. He tried to turn you in. Why would you reclaim a traitor?"

"That is not your concern. I just want him back."

"Fine. As you said, this complex is not my concern anymore. I'll give him to you, and I hope that you kill each other."

"Thank you."

The complex chief stops at the last door before the doctor offices and unlocks it. The door opens up to a new hallway with doors on both sides. I peek through the nearest door with a window and see a young girl strapped to a cot, squirming and crying. My heart goes out to her. Mr. Athill's voice pulls me away from the window. "Ah, here is your precious traitor. I hope that the battle between you two is bloody."

I roll my eyes. "You unstrap him. And let the little girl out too."

He glares at me. "I can't set a five-year-old free into the world."

"I know that, but you can at least take the straps off. She has rights now. Remember?"

His face becomes a blank slate. "Fine."

I check the other little cells to make sure there isn't anyone else being strapped against their will. There isn't anyone else in here. I walk in to the room with Jefrey and feel my pulse quicken as he opens his blue eyes and looks at me. "What are you doing here, Elira?" His eyes dim. "Were you captured?"

"No. We changed the law today." I feel tears of happiness, sadness, and maybe the beginnings of—forgiveness leaking down my cheeks. "We won. All of us are free."

He looks amazed for someone so heavily drugged. "Free?"

I put Shasta's arm around my neck when I see her drooping. "Yes. I rushed here as soon as the votes were in."

Jefrey takes a deep breath as the straps are released from his chest. A weird emotionless struggle happens on his face. "How can you stand to look at me—after what I did?"

"I—it's hard, Jefrey. I never would have done that to you, but—I love your brother and he wants you back, so I guess I can learn to deal with having you back too."

His eyes have so much less sparkle than his brother's. "Will you forgive me?"

I should but… "Avra almost died, Jefrey. We watched her lay unmoving for days."

He cringes. "I'm sorry. I have done nothing but regret what I did since I came back here. Please, forgive me." The complex chief looks at the two of us like we're crazy.

I pause for a moment and wonder how I'll feel if I don't forgive him. I'll probably have a cold, hard spot in my heart forever. —If I do forgive him, he may disappoint me and go back to his old ways—I'm tired of the hurt and pain of the last few months. I just want to feel warmth and love inside. I want my heart to be free of all cold spots so it can use its full capacity to—love.

I pull Jefrey to his feet after they've been unstrapped. "I don't think you deserve it, but I just want everyone, including myself, to start fresh right now. How can we show this country how to treat all people kindly if we don't do it ourselves? So—I forgive you."

Jefrey looks like he's crying without tears. I'm not sure if it's the pain in his limbs or what I just said. "Thank you, Elira. You have no idea how much I've wanted to hear you say that."

I put Jefrey on my other side so I can support both of my friends. When his arm touches Shasta's, she jumps in surprise. I remember that sensation. I turn to my boyfriend's twin. "Jefrey, don't betray me again, and we'll be able to get along." He nods without much energy, and we hobble slowly to the front doors with the complex chief sneering at us as we go.

Jefrey turns to me. "Where will I go?"

"I'll take you back to my parents' house."

His feet grind to a halt. "They hate me. I turned them in. It won't be safe for me there."

I raise my eyebrows at him. "Um, yeah, the boys might bash your face in, but where else would you go?"

"I don't know. My mom's maybe."

"Yeah, tomorrow. Tonight, you're coming with me."

The complex chief leads us to the door and surprisingly exits ahead of us without looking back. I guess he's done with this place too. The complex guards just stand there scratching their heads and watch us leave. When we get to the parking lot, Shasta needs help fitting her long, skinny body into Greggory's passenger seat. We have to slide the seat back as far as it will go. Jefrey manages to get himself in the seat behind me, but after he shuts the door he pauses. "Wait, you're driving?"

"Yep."

He buckles his seatbelt hurriedly. "Are you sure that's safe?"

And it starts already. "Save it, Jefrey. I'm tired of having this conversation with boys." As I step on the gas, Shasta looks at everything in and out of the car with wonder. "The air feels so cold, but it smells so fresh." She glues her eyes to the car window as we speed down the road. "Elira, where are we going?"

Good, she remembers me. I think she's snapping out of her stupor. "To my parents' house. Tomorrow we'll see if we can find your parents. Would you like that?"

She looks so confused. "My parents are alive?" She starts to shake. "I—I would just like to lay my head down and believe that there aren't toxins soaking into my skin."

Oh, boy. Where is Ernestine when I need her?

Chapter 31

"WHAT'S WRONG, ELIRA?" Jefrey asks as we pull up to my parents' house.

I have dreamed of this moment. I wipe the straggling tears off my face. "It feels like I haven't been here in forever. I've missed everyone so much."

Shasta looks at me questioningly. "Is this a house?"

I keep forgetting how little she knows. "Yes, Garth, Avra, and Scott are inside. Are you excited to see them again?"

She keeps looking at the light pole in awe. "I guess so." I'll be happy when all the drugs have left her system.

My heart just might beat its way out of my chest. Come

on, arms, I have to support three people's weight all the way to that front door. No more sneaking in the back, unless I want to. With Jefrey on one side of me and Shasta on the other, we waddle to the fancy main door. The door opens as we approach, and a frowning peace officer glares at us as he leaves. The silence is deafening after the door clicks shut. Huh, I guess no one inside saw us. "Push the doorbell, Jefrey."

He looks at me questioningly. "Isn't it after midnight?"

"Nobody is asleep in this house tonight. Push the dang doorbell!"

Ding dong. My heart positively explodes as the door opens and my parents, Ernestine, Rocky, Scott, Avra, and Garth burst through the door with smiles on their faces. As they wrap us in their arms, I feel more weight than Shasta and Jefrey being lifted from my shoulders. I'm home. And I'm free.

MY MOTHER AND FATHER shower me with hugs and kisses. They can't believe I stormed the complex tonight instead of waiting for Brock to take me. Garth isn't surprised though. He tells me as we break apart from our many kisses, "I knew you would go there and take them back. Did anyone try to stop you?"

I laugh as I remember the scene I caused. "Yeah, just two complex guards, the complex chief, and Mentor Roberta."

Garth pulls me out of the noisy entry way and into the hall. Shasta wanders like a lost soul behind me. My favorite person whispers in my ear, "I wouldn't stand in your way; I hope they learned their lesson." He kisses me in such a way that everyone in house must feel my joy. Well, everyone in the house except for Shasta. She is gasping and leaning against the wall for support.

I hug my boyfriend so tight, I can feel his heart syncing beats with mine. "Garth, this has been the hardest week of my life, but you were right, it was worth it. We're free!"

"WAHOO!" he screams. "I want to run through the streets of Herrington waving *both* of my hands in the air. Will you come with me?"

I laugh with more energy than I've ever had at midnight. "Yes! Let's go free Greggory too!"

He nods, but his eyes look unsure. "Okay, we can try. Do you think they'll let us take him?"

I smirk at him. "Have you listened to my story at all tonight? Who do you think I am?"

He smiles and brings me in for yet another kiss. "You're The Complex Leader."

About the Author

Heather Hayes loves a good story. She believes a good story will entertain you and leave you feeling like a better person for having read it. She loves living in Idaho with her husband and five daughters. If she isn't writing, she is probably watching a volleyball game, cooking, skiing, reading, or planning a trip to somewhere new.

A Message from Heather Hayes

If you liked following Elira's journey through her complex world, please tell your friends about it and leave a review on Amazon; it helps me out more than you know. Find more books by Heather Hayes on Amazon and HeatherHayesAuthor.com.

The Complex Life

The Complex Law

The Complex Leader

If you like a good story for younger readers, check out my other books:

Unexpected Magic

A Tale of Regrets

Rissy's Summer Son

The Fantastic Backyard of Imagination